Marc Phillips

The Legend of Sander Grant

TELEGRAM

London   San Francisco   Beirut

ISBN: 978-1-84659-064-1

Copyright © Marc Phillips 2009

This first edition published in 2009 by Telegram

A full CIP record for this book is available from the British Library.

Manufactured in Lebanon

TELEGRAM
26 Westbourne Grove, London W2 5RH
825 Page Street, Suite 203, Berkeley, California 94710
Tabet Building, Mneimneh Street, Hamra, Beirut
www.telegrambooks.com

For Bean. I'm speechless.

1

Sander is a giant. But people around Dixon are used to that. His daddy was a giant, and his daddy's dad, and so on. Back when other whites had just arrived, Sander's people were already there, and nobody knew where in all hell they came from. Those who used to trouble themselves about it, of course, they've grown old and died. Locals now remark on Sander Grant in the same way they do the August heat. Like a mother tells her kids Jesus is love. Sander is a giant.

The town of Dixon only exists relative to someplace else. It lacks noteworthy coordinates of its own and is thus defined – when it's mentioned at all – by proximity. East of Dallas. West of Louisiana. Across the Red River from Oklahoma and a grateful step behind the times. It's a good spot for cattlemen, land seemingly created by some bovine deity, and an ideal place for anyone content staying out of the public eye. The tight-knit community doesn't really conspire to keep secrets. It just so happens that rumors don't travel far through pine bark and country people won't say much worth hearing until the strangers leave.

The big men preferred their ranch outside of town. They ventured into Dixon proper as rarely as possible and were loath to stray across rural county lines. So they caused nary a stir for most of the twentieth century, in East Texas or beyond. Word of a Grant baby, meanwhile, never lost its curious appeal in those parts. It got people talking down at the feed store; over on the courthouse lawn; and up to Skinner's Meat Market where the subject naturally arose when locals bought Grant Beef. They kept talking as the child soared like a hemp weed, rapidly outgrowing a province tailored to regular folks and casting a shadow on any semblance of comfort around most of the folks themselves. Then he was simply another giant out at the Grant place and thereby restored the status quo.

Grant men favored small women, so the lore goes, none of recent memory being over five and a half feet. Who could know if that was a choice they made each on his own, or something they talked about father to son? This is what a lot of people in Dixon thought, that they were terribly pragmatic for the sake of their heirs, that they were breeding toward normalcy, managing their own bloodline like they managed that of their cattle. The fact that Sander and Dalton, his daddy, were as comfortable above their neighbors as the Texas sky didn't dissuade the ones prone to thinking such. How much sense would it make anyway, holding out for women their size?

Apart from their stature, the Grants were beautiful men. At least, the ones born since the advent of photographs. Even in nineteenth-century Tintypes, they exuded a nobility of which they were apparently unaware, which made them all the more attractive. None ever wanted for female companionship or, when the time came, a bride. Young women didn't complain over a giant's attention. Their parents did the bitching, generally with a bias toward forethought at the expense of youthful passion.

Josephine was eighteen when Dalton proposed to her. They had been dating for six short months. She carried home the news on a purling stream of emotion. Frank, her father, heard a call to the colors and took up the battle forthwith.

He told her, 'Jo, babe, you'll be looking after him all his life. They don't fit anywhere. It's no way to be. It's not meant to be.'

Doris said, 'Skip it, Frank. Can't you see the girl's in love?'

'Stop and think. It don't make no sense.'

Doris leaned into her daughter, 'Your poppy said the same thing to me about this one. "Find you another man. Can't you see how stupid he is?" It's what fathers do, honey. No man is good enough.'

Frank started to storm out of the kitchen in a huff, to brood in the garage like he used to do until somebody gave in. He made it only to the dining room table before he remembered supper was almost ready.

He sat down and said, 'Stupid don't eat a whole hog every other week or need special clothes sewed for his big ass, does he?'

'Tiresome just the same, though.'

'Doris, it aint a joke. Dalton's mother bled to death and she was nearly two of Jo. His father dropped dead at forty-five. Don't none of em live very long. Did he tell you that, Jo?'

'That's enough Frank. You said your piece.'

He raised some valid points, though none his daughter would hear. Brides truly paid a dire toll for having a Grant baby. Dalton's mother, Sandy, was a stout and formidable woman, but her body just couldn't tolerate the stress when he came out, three months early they say, and three feet long.

Frank knew his daughter wasn't asking his permission. Besides, she already had her mother's blessing. There was nothing more he could do, save further angering them both. The following autumn, when Jo was pregnant, his worst fears set upon him with terrible weight. Frank stopped sleeping for almost half a year. He could not be in the same room with Dalton for all that time.

Doctors knew more when Jo was big with Sander. When it got where she could barely stand, they opened her up and took Sander out. He'd been in there five months. The nurse wiped him off and stood him up, on his feet, to have a look at him. He wobbled a little as he watched the doctor cut his mother's spent uterus from her belly and dispose of it. The next month he was standing beside her at the kitchen sink, watching her peel potatoes.

When his daughter didn't die, and once it was medically impossible for her to give birth again, Frank latched onto Sander and wouldn't hardly allow the boy room to breathe. He had to be told to let him alone sometimes, to quit cleaning his face and pampering him, let him go get scraped up, get into some poison ivy, fall off a fence, and generally be a boy. Doris rode her husband about his smothering tendencies. Then, when he wasn't looking, she gave Sander sweet things she baked especially for him and she cooed to him and measured him for something nice she was always making. She asked him how much bigger he thought he'd be in three weeks when she finished this sweater, or these pajamas.

They started regular Sunday dinners at Jo's parents' house. Frank insisted on it, and Doris would not allow them to bring any food.

'I can feed my children,' she told them, 'one day a week. Let me.'

Dalton couldn't get comfortable anywhere, but he didn't say a word about it. He sat on the floor in the living room or a low ottoman at one end of their table and smiled at Jo.

Doris cooked in jumbo stock pots that would fit whole turkeys and arranged food in great mounds on the table. She dared the fellas to eat it all. They never quite did. There was always a slice of meatloaf left, a few rolls, one scoop of beans that would be put away for leftovers. And when Jo got her family home afterward, she would pull two briskets and a casserole out of the oven. She would pat them on their backs as they sat down to finish eating and she would tell them they were so kind to her folks.

On their way out to their truck one Sunday, Frank grabbed Dalton by the waist of his pants and pulled him aside. He looked up and said, 'Don't you let nobody tease him. You hear? And you keep him fed.' He said it like he was prepared to whip his son-in-law's ass if he didn't take heed.

'I promise, Frank.'

But if Sander needed shelter from anything, it was Josephine doing the sheltering. The sweet little bride turned into a she-bear when it came to her boy. People figured since she gave up part of her insides to have him, she'd be damned if anybody was gonna harm him. It's why Sander long ago quit claiming any rights to his given name. In the presence of his mother, nobody ever used it. They grew accustomed to Jo saying, 'Where's my boy?' 'My boy will help me with that.' And, at the Affiliated Grocery as folks watched her empty the freezer into her cart, 'My boy likes his chicken.' They took to calling him Jo's boy.

You hardly saw him with his daddy. Dalton was a busy man. The more he took on himself, the less hired help he needed with the ranch. In addition, none of his people were ever given to colorful expressions of their inner thoughts and feelings. So it might have seemed to the unknowing eye that, though the Grant men had a core goodness you could bank on, they weren't an especially caring lot. That couldn't be further from the truth. It was said about Dalton, as with his father Will, that you could trust completely whatever understanding it seemed like you had with the Grants – but don't expect it to be hashed out in discussion. This held true for family. There simply wasn't that much talking, yet the care these men took was tender, in all things.

Grant Beef was the family business and ambassador of the family philosophy. The brand has been around for quite a while now. At first, the talk of the new ranch was, 'What else are giants going to do? They won't fit indoors.' Then, 'They have a natural way with those cows. It's uncanny.' And now they say, 'Yeah, this is a damn good steak, but you can tell it's not Grant Beef.'

Over the one hundred and seventy-five years represented in the ranch books, you can trace the meticulous development of hybrid Angus/Simmental stock known across the nation as Grant's. In those pages, you would see the chronicled history of superior cattle ranching, the building of a new brand from a paltry ten head and nearly two centuries of sweat. And then there are the things you won't see in the books. Not a single missed day. No terse notes in a tired, sloppy hand. No tiny detail or mild concern left out. For an unbroken chain of 63,692 days, dawn to dusk, these enormous men coaxed out of Dixon pastures the only statement they felt germane regarding life, love, and obligation.

Actually, you wouldn't see any of that. Not a glimpse. Possibly someone could've raised a mob to subdue Dalton, ransacked that huge house, and might've found the books. Barring that, nobody saw those books. Texas A&M University had been writing for three decades, pleading the case for higher learning, offering interns to help on the ranch, free visits from their top vets in exchange for some inside knowledge of the operation. No deal. Will's father told him, Will told Dalton, and Dalton would soon pass it along to Sander. 'Grant cattle comes from Grant land. Nowhere else. It's ours. Protect it.'

The hired hands bailed hay, helped with the worming, branding, barn and tractor maintenance and the like. That's it. They were not involved in cutting the herd, culling, sizing up brood cows from the new heifers, and never allowed near the bulls alone.

By 1980, Dalton had built back up to eight bulls that showed promise as herd sires. He separated and fenced them off in different tracts spread over the twelve hundred acres. He had space ready for half a dozen more when the right genes cropped up. He had recently survived a horrifying lesson, not long after taking over the ranch himself. He learned that even in the most careful of operations, calamity visited.

The summer drought of '69 killed two bulls and heat stroke sterilized another. In '75, a stray .30-30 round from a hunter's rifle struck and slew Buster Bingham, the long-time senior bull, maybe the best in fifty years. Lightning took Buster's heir apparent the following spring. Another prize sire would not distinguish himself for two generations, and Dalton swore not to be the first Grant to compromise the line, so the herd numbers steadily fell during those years leading up to 1976, the year he wed Josephine.

In bed one night, not many weeks after their vows, she listened to the rotten luck that had befallen him of late and she said, 'Maybe it's time you talk to God and see won't He throw us a break, so we can get our feet under us. He likes married people.'

'Does He?'

'Yes. Or He approves of it, as a rule.'

'I don't know that I could be civil right this minute. I'm a little scared.'

'I can tell, sweetie.' She kissed him on the forehead. 'I'll do it for you. Don't worry.' And they conceived Sander.

God took His time in getting back to Jo, but she could be patient like a river rock when the mood struck her. She had other things on her mind, what with Sander kicking around in there. Dalton kept busy with the beef sales, rationing, rotating to different markets, driving up the price to compensate for falling production. He willed his young bulls to grow, to show him the traits he needed to see, and he didn't press Jo for a response from the Lord.

Sander was born and, for a short time, he and his mamma were the only concern around that house. Then the troubles came back. Over the following months, the stress began etching lines on Dalton's forehead, around his eyes and mouth. Jo felt his big shoulders turn to knotted *bois d'arc* timbers under the strain.

It was the early winter of '78 when she finally had enough. A belligerent, relentless cold spell like no one alive had witnessed threatened to wrack the herd. Her man was poring over the books at the kitchen table, groaning and shaking his head, seeing his imminent failure written there. The sun had set and the house was haunted with quiet exasperation. Sander sat on the sofa and stared at his kneecaps. He would look around tentatively and look down again without comment. He couldn't know that life was not like this, that these were only rough times, that he wouldn't feel this way all his life. He had not been among them a full year.

She saw that her child was nervous in his own home, and Jo couldn't tolerate that. He needed to keep busy at something until they sorted this out. She bundled her son in his heaviest coat and sent him out back to stack wood on the patio.

'It's night-time mamma.'

'Turn on the light.'

'Can I split some?'

'You stay away from that axe. Now go.'

She wrapped herself in a bathrobe and scarf, put her fluffy house slippers on, and walked out the front door. She eased it shut so Dalton didn't look up and wonder at the foolishness of what she was doing. Snow began to fall. Shattery flakes lit in her red hair, covered freckles on her face and perched on her eyelashes. She walked far enough to allow some privacy, turned her head up and told God she'd come to talk.

Back in the kitchen, Dalton got hungry. He put away the books and called for Jo. No answer. He found his son out there at the woodpile and went to ask him where his mamma was. The boy didn't know, which was odd. He always knew. As they stood there staring at one another, shivering, Dalton heard Jo's voice coming over the second-story roof from the front yard.

'You look here! You will step up and do Your job. Help my man. Are You listening to me?'

Dalton said, 'Go inside, boy.'

And he followed his son. They stood silent in the kitchen, sharing a loaf of white bread and a gallon of milk. They could thankfully hear only the murmuring crescendos of the argument outside. Then thunder began to roil in the winter night, low and slow, and shook the rafters above them when it cracked. Sander spoke up first.

'Is she praying, daddy?'

'I believe she's dressing Him down, son. I don't recommend trying it yourself.'

'No sir.'

Sander was tucked into bed when his mother came back inside. Her face was blotchy from the cold. Dalton stood and waited.

'Well?' he asked her.

'It's time to put my boy in school next year. I'll take care of that.' She dried melting snow from her hair with a dishtowel. 'Breed your two youngest bulls in the spring. They'll do for now. Nut all the yearlings except the blackest. Meanwhile, take the herd down to three hundred head, no further. Can you do that?'

'Yeah.'

'And don't look for God around here for a while. We're on the outs, but He'll get over it.'

The following Monday, Jo took her boy down to the Superintendent's office at Dixon Independent School District. Sander had to pass a battery of tests since, at next enrollment date he would be only two years old, but they eventually let him into kindergarten.

Dalton took heed of her advice in the pastures. Bringing to bear all his knowledge of breeding and skill in stock management, he was hopeful he might even keep the herd above three hundred fifty head. Week after week, things were looking up. So much so, on occasion Jo lamented to her mother that she could have but one of Dalton's children. How she wanted a sister for her boy. Her mother warned her not to ever let her boy hear that. He would take it wrong.

'I know, mom.'

'Nor your pop. He loves Sander to death, but I see him cringe sometimes and I can tell he's thinking of that boy coming out of you.'

Dalton also spoke to his father, Will. Actually, he spoke to four generations of his ancestors. They were all deceased, and

Will's voice was the only one audible to Dalton, but that did little to dampen the conversations.

One Saturday that fall, he sat atop the family grave, beneath a live oak atop a hill and overlooking the largest pond in their north pasture, his five feet of legs stretched out before him. It was the rarest of sights, a Grant man in repose while the sun shone. He plucked dandelions and chewed sourweed and fidgeted like a child. Made small talk. At last he worked up to blurting it out. He told his daddy he intended to freeze sperm as soon as he found the right bull. He didn't know if he could say all this to the old man amid interruptions, so he spilled his whole plan, reasons and argument, in a rushing stream.

He would hire professionals from Elgin Breeding Service over in Bastrop County. The best in the business. He would pay whatever to have them come here and teach him how to collect the semen, and he would watch them every second. He would have them recommend a freezer and all the equipment needed to keep it safe and viable. Every drop accounted for in the books. He felt he only needed to say once that he would not, under any circumstance, sell the Grant bloodline, but the fact was, these past few years, disaster had come too close for comfort. He was sure he could keep a dozen heifers alive no matter what, worse come to worst, and if he had some semen stored, he could always start over.

The major risk was theft. Grant Beef brought nearly triple the price of common stock. It was gold on four legs. People had long since been trying to steal a young bull from their pastures, especially during Will's day. Back then, horsemen riding the fence line with rifles numbered as many as all the other ranch hands combined. Not as much a worry these days, but the bulls were still kept in the center of the spread. Then again, semen is roughly four hundred and ninety-seven pounds lighter than one of their weaned calves. He had taken all this into consideration. The storage facility would be a vault. There would be one key, which he would eventually hand over to Sander.

That was it. Dalton's considerable thinking on the subject, in short. He waited. The wind shifted and blew his hair into his face. He thought he might need to add more about how perilously close he had come to pissing away the legacy. Maybe frame some of his ideas as questions. He suddenly felt disrespectful and insubordinate.

Will said, 'He's quite a boy. You done good, son. And a family name you gave him. Thanks for that. Your mother would be so proud. He looks like Sandy's father, you know it?'

'Yeah. The name was Jo's idea. She wouldn't have it any other way. She likes us.'

'She takes good care of you?'

'Yes daddy, she does.'

'She's a fine woman.'

'The best.'

'But she scares hell out of me sometimes.'

'Me too.'

Then his father told him, 'You'll do what you think is best to keep the herd. I wouldn't have left it to you if I didn't trust that. Stand strong. Bring my grandbaby to see me.'

'Yes sir. When he's ready.'

2

The world awaiting Sander at Gardner Elementary School was not the one he expected. His parents did not discuss it with him at length, so he had no basis to expect anything. Since when, though, does a child need any basis to see a future of his making?

As the end of summer approached and the first day of kindergarten along with it, Jo would bring up the subject when they were alone. This was odd and uncomfortable to Dalton, her asking for his thoughts on this stuff. He preferred Jo rule the house and matters thereabout in the manner which had thankfully become her custom, as an unyielding matriarch, benevolent but noticeably absent due process. This, he was certain, was the bedrock of their strength as a family. Meanwhile, he plied the land which fed them, his domain and birthright, with fathoms of understanding from Grant generations before him and, on occasion, with arms that could nudge a hillside back in line when it was justified. It seemed the proper order of things. The vestiges of medieval order hadn't faded so much among Dalton's people. They had always served at the behest of their Queen.

The first time his wife said, 'I have no idea how to prepare him for this, do you?'

He told her, 'I only have the one child too, Jo,' and he kept his further opinions on the subject to himself.

He could feel she was already seeing, thirteen years down the road, the boy graduating in cap and gown, with smiles, tears, *Pomp and Circumstance*. She was trying to anticipate all the bumps and hurdles along that road. Dalton didn't envision such a long journey. Graduation hadn't proven workable for him. He ended his public schooling in the fourth grade – when he was seven feet tall – and his maternal grandmother took up that part of his education. His father taught him other things. Conformity issues tended to sort themselves out as they saw fit and, in his experience, it had not made any difference what worrying he applied.

But later, lying beside him in their bed, she wanted to know, 'What was it like for you?'

'Strange,' he said, 'but not unpleasant.'

'How did your dad– What did he say to you when you were starting school?'

'Grandma said I would do well in whatever I tried, and daddy told me not to get it in my head that school meant I didn't have to do my chores anymore.'

'Is that what you intend to say to my boy?'

'I hadn't intended to say anything. He already knows as much, just like I did. I wish you wouldn't fret so much over this. He's a good person. People will like him. They'll want to keep him, and he needs to feel that.'

Jo sat bolt upright and turned on the lamp. 'Well they can't have him.'

When he didn't respond, she said, 'They can't have him. Do you understand me?'

'Yes. He's yours, honey.'

But that was not nearly enough reassurance. So, when the first morning of school came, Sander's mother left him with some choice words of her own to recall.

'Come back to me.'

'I will, mamma.'

Sander brought home his stories of this new place as though none had been there before him and Jo studied her boy carefully as he regaled her. Mixed with his wonder and curiosity were traces of disappointment. The selfish part of her reveled in that. The majority of her wanted more for him, wanted him to like it too much, for a while at least. It was a month before Ms Moffit called the house.

'He's a real treat to have in my class, but he's terribly bored, Mrs Grant. I try to spend time with him, answering his questions and giving him things to do, but it takes away from time I should be spending with the rest of the kids. It's not fair to him or them.'

'What do we do, then?'

'I spoke with the counselor and the principal. Sander's test scores are high enough to bump him to the first grade, but his emotional development is more second-grade level. Could you and your husband come in for a conference?'

'Yes. I can, anyway.'

'Also. You should know this. Your boy has a tremendous talent for painting. You might think of having someone more knowledgeable than me look at his work.'

So Sander finished that year in the first grade and this started a pattern of skipping a grade every so often – when the boredom threatened to return – that would follow him throughout grammar school. At first, the obvious practical difficulties with this were addressed by the school counselor, who came up with the idea of sending Sander home for the summer with the books from the grade he would likely skip. She told Jo that the things children learn in the lower grades are not difficult to master. They spread them out over several years to keep pace with the maturity level of average children, their attention spans more than their aptitude. Sander had plenty of attention to give, she said, and it shouldn't take much of Jo's time to prepare him to skip the early grades. However, she suggested a summer tutor once he passed grade six.

It worked wonderfully for a good while. Sander was a blissfully happy four-year-old headed into the third grade the next fall with high marks. Jo marveled at her boy's intelligence, loved spending summers teaching him, and would go back to school herself or whatever it took to be able to keep things the way they were until he finished school. She wasn't at all inclined to delegate this experience to any tutor. Dalton was happy because his family seemed happy.

Then the less obvious concern emerged. It was less obvious to Jo because she longed to be everything her boy required in a companion. Sander made no friends in the crowd of chattering, giggling little people scurrying around him because he couldn't talk to them. But he made no enemies either. He got along much better with the teachers, that's all. As he developed physically, the younger male teachers in the elementary school had to fight the urge to invite him over for a beer some weekend. The young women secretly wondered how much a kid he could truly be, square-jawed, powerful, and well-spoken as he was. While the kids, they said only, 'Pick me up, Sander!', 'Swing me!', 'Bet you can't lift this thing.' He learned to politely ignore them.

Doris told her daughter again and again that it could not continue that way. It wasn't healthy. The child had to have friends. He needed to find out firsthand how to interact with his peers.

'His peers are wetting the bed and eating crayons, mom.'

'You know what I mean. He'll be out in the real world in the blink of an eye, running that ranch himself and ...'

'Not if you let him on the football team, he won't.'

'Shut up, Frank.' Then, to her daughter, 'Sweetheart, long-term relationships can't be taught. Not by a mother at least. He has to be able to deal with people. What will he do for friends, skipping grades like that?'

Art provided the answer. Jo smiled at the thought of her boy wielding a paintbrush, expressing himself on canvas, ever since Ms Moffit told her of Sander's flair for it. She had an easel set up in one of the spare bedrooms and he spent long hours at it. As with all his subjects, he craved every scrap of knowledge available to him. His parents hadn't an artistic bone in their bodies, so Jo found herself hiring a tutor for Sander after all. He was Jason Markette, a twenty-three-year-old painter with a studio in town. He had shown his work all over Texas and twice in New York. Sort of a local celebrity, this young man.

As with most artists, despite his burgeoning notoriety, Jason wasn't exactly flush with cash, so he jumped at the offer of a steady gig working with Sander once a week at their home. The spare bedroom with an easel became a full-fledged studio. Paint on the floor, music at odd hours, and the essence of spirits on still air. Jason was respectful and patient with his student. He initially treated Sander like a job. Then he reacted to him as a child. Within a year, it was something else.

Once a week tutoring became twice a week. Those were the paid visits. Jason visited more often as Sander progressed and diverged from his teacher's style. They talked in a rapid banter. They argued. They insulted and praised one another. Physically, they were the same size. They had a common wit. Their laughter sometimes grated on Dalton's nerves.

While Jo actively schemed to heed her mother's advice – taking her boy to the park and playgrounds and the mall, urging him to socialize with other kids he'd passed in school, and those he would soon catch – Sander had found his own friend in Jason, who was a mere three years younger than Jo. Initially, this seemed to bear out Dalton's doctrine of life as a giant. Let things sort themselves out, you know. Yet, oddly enough, he was the first to feel the itch of resentment.

He hid it well. He knew it was selfish, but when they began working more and more alongside one another in the pastures, he did not especially like Sander coming out with thoughts that sounded as though they should be spoken by Jason. Some were prefaced that way: 'Jason says ...' Some were not, but they were Jason's nonetheless. The man had an annoying habit of speaking in parables.

The danger with parables is in how they're interpreted by the teller, and how that interpretation is passed along to the listener. Dalton knew this, but he fought to keep his mouth shut and chalk it up to part of Sander's education. Growing up. He made an admirable job of it until, shortly after his son's eighth birthday, Jason taught the boy how to shave. Dalton was upset with Jason over that and he told his wife so.

'Now you sound like me,' Jo told him. 'We can't teach him everything. He'll pick things up as he goes along.'

'What else is he picking up from Jason? I'm saying what do we know about this guy?'

'We know he makes my boy happy. He can paint, we know that. Have you looked at what your son is doing? It's beautiful.'

'Yes, I have. I think it's great. But have you looked at how he's dressing? The things he says? It doesn't seem like him sometimes. Sounds a lot like religious talk if you ask me.'

'Religion strikes you as foolish now.'

'No, honey, it doesn't. I'm wondering if you wouldn't rather be the one to teach that to your boy is all.'

'Do I come out there and tell you how to build a fence?'

'Not lately.'

'Not once. Let me take care of what goes on in here.'

'Will you at least find out where Jason's from? Please.'

Jo was angrier with her husband than she let on. He didn't figure it out until supper that evening. Dalton had always hated beans: beans in general, but specifically limas, pintos, garbanzos, and navy beans. They were the only things you could put on a plate that would raise a complaint from him. After lunch, Jo made a special trip to the grocery store. Supper that night was five-bean salad, pinto and bacon soup, navy beans with rice, and there could have been beans in the pudding for dessert.

'This is so good, mamma. We never have beans. Why don't we eat beans more? Jason says beans are brain food.'

'I'm glad you like it, hon. We might just have them more often. You never know.'

Dalton ate what he could stand and went to bed with a growling wildcat in his stomach. In addition to unintentionally pissing off his wife, he had also succeeded more than he could know in sewing a nagging concern inside her. She began that night cataloging the things she knew of Jason. There wasn't much. She thought about his lean, wiry figure and unkempt appearance, which she had previously chalked up to the persona of an artist. Did she want her boy to be like that? She remembered that she had smelled smoke on Jason more than once and now she worried that Sander would show up with cigarettes. Or worse. The local news ran stories now and then about designer drugs popping up at parties and football games in Dixon. More and more with every passing day, Sander was looking like a grown man, and acting like one. Still, eight years old is too young to lock horns with serious vice. Maybe he should be riding horses more while they could carry him, and painting a little less.

Jo decided she would check into Jason Markette, find out something more about him than the fact that people seemed to like his work. If what she discovered was benign or irrelevant, she would never tell her boy she'd been snooping. If it went the other way, she'd deal with that when it arose. This marked the first secret she had ever actively kept from Sander, and she didn't like the feel of it. But she could do this no other way.

For his part, Dalton was formulating a plan. Not so much a plan to meddle; rather, he determined he'd made some mistakes as a father and would set about methodically correcting them. First, it was past the time for Sander to be taking more responsibility over the herd. Will had given Dalton a paid part-time job on the place when he was six. How this had slipped Dalton's mind on Sander's sixth birthday he did not know. This very day, a Saturday, when the oversight occurred to him, Dalton dropped a willow tree he had plucked from the bank of the creek, took off his gloves and walked back to the house. He found his son alone, upstairs in the studio.

'Where's your mother?'

Without turning from the canvas, Sander said, 'Went to town. An hour or so ago.'

'Hey. How does ten dollars an hour sound to you?'

'Do what?' Now he looked at his daddy.

'Ten dollars an hour, twenty hours a week. That's fair, aint it? Eight hundred dollars a month, working for your old man.'

'Yes sir, it's fair. But I don't know that I want a regular job at this juncture.'

'What juncture? I don't know that I'm asking you what you want. You can work five four-hour days, or six threes and a two. It's up to you. You start tomorrow.'

'Tomorrow is Sunday. Jason comes on Sunday.'

'Monday then.' Sander nodded at him. 'That's your best work yet, by the way.' He pointed at the canvas.

Sander studied it. 'Jason says it's stilted and trite. My colors are muddled to hide inexperience. I might need to trash it.'

'Don't trash it before your mother sees it. Please.' He would've liked to muddle Jason's colors a bit right then. Something occurred to Dalton. 'Isn't Sunday the Sabbath?'

'If God made all days, then they all belong to him. He wouldn't expect us to live in modern times by the same rules as ancient societies, daddy.'

'I see. It's good none of that stuff is written in stone, then.'

On his way back across the pasture, a second thing struck Dalton. It was time Sander learned to drive. This wasn't as glaring a misstep as the job, because it hadn't been an issue with Dalton and his daddy. Will didn't have a truck that would fit him. He went the places he needed to go in his old ranch cart hitched to a two-horse team. There weren't that many places he needed to go. Now though, Dalton did have a Ford crew cab pick-up with the front seats bolted where the back seats had been removed. It wasn't comfortable or stylish, but it worked. He always saw his father as somewhat limited by his size, his lack of independence. He didn't want his son feeling that way. And, if he were able to get out and around from time to time, he might meet other interesting people, pick up some things from them to balance out the Jason monopoly.

This is something which surely had to be discussed with Jo, which got him thinking. Where had Jo gone? She didn't tell him anything about running errands this morning.

He was nearly to the creek. The willow was all muddy now, spanning the water like a felled bridge. He wished he had carried it to a clearing at least, instead of letting it smack down in the soggy muck. He took his gloves from his back pocket and looked at them. Buckskin. Great gloves, his favorite pair. The first few pairs Jo made were beautiful, but there was something about the fit that weakened his grip when he wore them. They were not quite right. Jo noticed the calluses on his hands growing. They scratched her, and she knew he wasn't wearing his gloves. Without saying anything to him about it, she sat at her sewing machine and made one new pair a day and handed them to him as he walked through the door in the evening. She would tell him to put them on.

'Make a fist,' she'd say. He would and she turned his hands this way and that, feeling for tight spots, tugging on loose spots. Then, 'Okay, take them off.' The next day it was the same thing. This went on for a week, until he put on a pair of gloves identical to these and they fit around his hands like water. He couldn't help smiling. She told him he'd have to go one more day without them while she made a pattern. Then he'd never be without gloves again. And he better wear them.

As he slipped on this pair, he was looking north at the top of the hill by the stock tank. He thought about what he told his daddy. Jo did take care of him. She was more woman than a sane man would expect. He knew his daddy had to be anxious to talk to his grandson. He had planned to let Sander adjust to the low-set reality around him for a little longer, until he was maybe ten, before he introduced the two. It was a danger for them, getting so wrapped up in their strangeness that they couldn't relate to anything normal. He saw the world enveloping his son at a much faster rate than any generation before, and he so wanted this for Sander. Yet, he wanted him to take the Grant heritage along with him. Now the greater danger seemed to be Sander picking up notions that those things which made him different were somehow wrong.

So far as Dalton knew, the way of his people wasn't exactly at odds with the teachings of any religion. Then again, few were privy to their ways, and the Grants had not been inside a church for generations. None of his forefathers had actually studied the Bible, any version of it, since before they came to Texas. Possibly they had ages ago sworn off mythology and the sundry Christian writings because they were there and knew how little of it was accurate. Though, had Dalton ventured a few chapters into the *Good Book*, he might also have guessed they cast it aside from sheer horror.

The knowledge Dalton had of the *Word of God* was rudimentary at best, anecdotal. He figured it was likely what most Christians knew of the text, instead of what they claimed to know. The burr in his brain now was more instinctual, however, a nameless and nagging uneasiness over Sander's determined foray into such matters. He resolved to show his son more truth about his own kind before any lies took foothold in the boy. He would bring Sander to his grandfather's hill soon, and they would talk, the three of them. He didn't have to run this one by Jo.

Once more, where was Jo? Somewhere. He would find out soon enough. There was a lot of work left to do today, and it wouldn't be put off any longer.

3

'Josephine! My goodness, girl. I haven't seen you for a coon's age. You've been hiding from us.' This from Doll, the reigning gossip in town, owner of Doll House Thrift and Antiques.

How to do this, Jo thought, so it won't be glaringly obvious? She made big eyes at an atrocious, yellowing, second-hand wedding dress displayed on a mannequin near the sidewalk window. She felt the lace neckline and fought a shiver. This should be on the dried corpse of a widow woman, rotting under the red clay.

'I've been busy, is all. Nobody told me mothering was a twenty-four-hour job. But it's girl's day out today. This is gorgeous, Doll. If I had a daughter ... How much are you asking?'

'Hon, if you had a daughter, that would make a darling little toddler outfit for her to play dress-up with. Let me get a look at you.' Doll's hands were old and spotted, but incredibly strong, like talons gripping Jo's shoulders. 'Are you losing weight?'

'I don't think so, but maybe. Good of you to notice.'

'It's not a compliment, honey. You need to eat. Where's your big man today?'

She pulled Jo to the quilting table in the rear of the store while another woman was meandering through the racks, shopping like someone listening to every peep around her. 'I saw you last, let's see, about a year after your boy was born. We were so worried for you. So worried. How is he?'

'Fine. They're both fine. Out at the ranch.'

'Have a seat. Take a load off. Are they eating you out of house and home?'

The other shopper was now rifling through scarves and old silver earrings at the end of the table where they sat.

'Those are already sold. Sorry,' Doll told her. The woman sighed and left. 'Well?' she asked Jo. 'Is it what you thought it would be, living with giants?'

'I wish you wouldn't say that. They're already sensitive enough about it.'

That was a lie, but Jo hoped it might unbalance Doll. Everyone knew you didn't come here for the company. You either have a little something to hang on the grapevine, or you're hungry to pick something off it. Generally, it's an even exchange. Jo was hoping she wouldn't have to give up much, as she hated gossiping and didn't know much of it besides. This is haggling. She needed to maintain the upper hand.

'That was vulgar, wasn't it? Forgive an old lady.'

'It's alright. I know people are curious. We're all doing very well these days. Thanks for asking. The herd is back up, and all this rain we've been having has Dalton about ready to sacrifice a fatted calf to the gods in thanks.' She chuckled.

'Gods?'

'I'm kidding, Doll. It is nice, though, when things are looking up. Not having to worry so much about bills. Speaking of which,' said Jo, doing her best to make it sound offhanded, 'I have to pay Sander's tutor. I think his studio is right over here.'

'The artist?'

'Yeah, Jason. Do you know him?'

'Not personally. He's bisexual, but I guess you already knew that.'

'How would I know that, exactly?'

'Everybody does, hon. It's no big secret. Haven't you seen his work? Gracious. He paints peckers nearly as much as anything. You can't paint peckers that good unless you've seen a few. And the drugs. Put two and two together. To each his own, I reckon.'

Right. What a rancid old crone this woman is. Jo could imagine what they talked about in here regarding her boy's friendship with Jason. Wenches.

'Artists paint nudes all the time, Doll. It doesn't necessarily mean they're gay.'

'What about artists who have sleepovers with other men and kiss them on the mouth in the Dairy Queen? Does that mean they're gay? Besides, I said bisexual. He's had women up there too. I think they're from that church he goes to where they beat on drums and dance around.'

'I reckon it means something. It's news to me. Did you say drugs?'

'Oh yes. He has a record. You should really check references more, Jo. People figured you knew these things. I said maybe you didn't, but ...'

'Where?'

'Do what?'

'Where does he have a criminal record?'

'I can't say for sure. Says he comes from San Diego. But that doesn't sound like a San Diego accent, does it? Sounds suspiciously like Little Rock to me.'

A woman and her teenaged daughter walked in. The door chime rang and Doll steered the topic of conversation in another direction.

'So, how's your boy's painting coming along?'

'Great. I couldn't be happier.' Actually, at that particular instant, Jo couldn't breathe. She wondered what to do with this information, and where all the oxygen had gone.

A question came from the front of the store. Jo didn't catch what it was, but Doll was standing up to see to her customers.

Jo said, 'I've got some more running around to do. I'll catch up with you later.'

'Okay, hon. Don't be a stranger.'

Jo started walking. It didn't matter which direction. It was the mindless rhythm of the act she needed, not so much to get anywhere. She strode down the sidewalk until it ended on the south side of the square. She turned and walked west, in front of Walgreens, past the vacant building that read Dollar General on the storefront, and came to the end of the line again facing Mail Boxes Etc. Looking directly across the square, she saw the dome of the old stone courthouse. Two blocks behind the courthouse was Jason's studio, and above it, his loft.

Screw this private eye nonsense, she thought. She would go straight over and ask him some questions. She had a right. She was a mother. At what point had she forgotten that little tidbit? If the son of a bitch had given her boy any drugs, she'd stomp a mud hole in his ass and walk it dry.

Jason answered his door wearing blue jeans and nothing else. His torso was covered in paint splatters and he looked as though he'd just rolled out of bed. He wore a silver chain around his neck with a stylized crucifix pendant. Jo had never noticed it before, but doubted it was new.

'Mrs Grant. This is a surprise. Is anything wrong?'

'No. Well, I don't know. Can I ...' She pointed past him.

'Come in, please. Excuse the mess.'

She sat on the sofa and he offered her hot herbal tea, choice of five flavors. How very California chic of him. He took a stained white shirt from the back of his chair and put it on.

'Hot tea? No. I'm hot already from walking. Thanks. You don't have a Coke or something, do you?'

'Sorry. I don't drink caffeine anymore, so I don't keep it around. And the milk has turned to cream. Water?'

'Yes, please.'

Bringing it back, he said, 'You look stressed. What's up?'

'I don't know anything about you, Jason. Other than you don't drink caffeine.'

'And it bothers you suddenly. That you don't know. What have you heard? Wait. That's a bad way to start, defensive. Let me tell you some about me and you can compare it to what you heard.' He took a deep breath and ran his fingers through his oily hair. 'I don't drink caffeine because they taught us in Narcotics Anonymous what the stuff does to your body. I was in Narcotics Anonymous because it was a condition of my parole. I was paroled because – or partially because – I taught art lessons in prison. Evidence of rehabilitation. I was in prison because I had become convinced that drugs were either an inspiration for, or an unavoidable side effect of my art. It's a more common misconception than you would probably believe.' He stood and said, 'I'm going to need my tea to continue this conversation. Excuse me for a moment?'

Jo took a sip of her water, placed the glass on the table and turned to stare out the window as Jason disappeared into the kitchen. The beep of the microwave filled the small loft and left in a rush through some invisible opening. The space was quieter then than it had been before. A clock ticked somewhere in the kitchen. Jason's knees creaked when he sat down in the chair and a spring somewhere within the worn cushions twanged.

'Been up all night working. If I appear dim-witted or rude this morning, that's my excuse.'

'It's afternoon.'

He looked out the window.

'So it is. Morning to me. I've forgotten which part of my sordid past we were passing judgment on when I left off. Where was I?'

Jo wouldn't do that, make it easy for him to be flippant by giving him any comment. She looked him square in the eye until he continued.

'I made ignorant choices like all children do, Mrs Grant. The difference being, I was called on the carpet for mine. Arrested for possession of marijuana and amphetamines. I had a sufficient amount to distribute, so that's what they charged me with. I did eighteen months and my parole was up shortly before I moved here.'

'From where?'

'San Diego. I was a Junior at San Diego State at the time. Art scholarship.'

'Is that where your folks are?'

'My parents are dead, but I'm originally from Texarkana, on the Arkansas side. I have a sister and two aunts there. I wanted to be close to them. I settled on Dixon. A long enough drive to make surprise pop-ins unlikely, but not long enough to give me an excuse to lose touch. My stupidity devastated them, financially and emotionally. I came out of prison with two things. Motivation, which came from the knowledge that my luck and time were running out, and these tattoos, which I did myself, from boredom.' He rubbed his hand across his belly.

'Those are tattoos?'

'You thought I never washed the paint off myself. Seems like that's what I wanted people to think when I did them. Because, spiritually, I don't. A sort of reminder to myself as well, of what I should be doing every waking moment.'

'What happened to your parents?'

'Plain Jane car wreck. There's no dirt there.'

'Stop it, Jason. Call this a belated job interview, or call it a mother's prerogative, but don't you make me into a snoop and a gossip. It's because I'm not those things that I never heard of your past before now. We've been good to you.'

'You have. What else would you like to know?'

'When is the last time you did drugs?'

'The morning of the day I went to prison. Not inside, and not since. There've been plenty of chances. Don't doubt it. Even here. I've talked to Sander about it. I share my daily victories over it in hopes he'll see what a struggle it is once you start down that path. I think it's helpful, but I'll stop if you want.'

'What else have you shared with him?'

'I'm sorry?'

'What do you talk about other than painting and drugs?'

They stared into one another for the second time. Several slow ticks rattled out of the unseen clock.

'Philosophy. That's the big one. There's no end to his curiosity. Girls, of course. Growing up. I tell him what it's like being a small man, and he tells me what it's like not. I have to admit I'm fascinated by him physically, but I try not to dwell.'

'Has it gone any further than fascination?'

'As an artist, I meant. Your son is not gay.'

'And your religion. Is that something else you picked up in prison?'

'My cellmate introduced me to the *Word* and gave me some food for thought. I couldn't come to terms with the pastor, though, so I wasn't saved until I got out. My faith could've been such a tremendous help to me inside, but I didn't have it then.'

'I appreciate your honesty. You won't come over tomorrow. I have some thinking to do. I'll call you early in the week.' She stood.

'Wait. There's something else I've talked over with Sander. We were going to discuss it with you and Mr Grant tomorrow. Will you sit a while longer, please?' She sat. 'I've witnessed to him. Because he asked me. He's seen God's influence in my work and … it was unavoidable. Not that I would avoid it. I strongly believe it's a good thing and I know you agree.'

'You know I agree?'

'Sander says you never go to church as a family, but he's heard you talking to the Lord. Our congregation wants to invite your family to worship at First Unitarian.'

'You talk about my family at your church?'

'We pray for you all the time. And the Lord speaks to Roger.' He saw the question in Jo's eyes and said, 'Roger Carlson is our pastor.'

'Yeah. Well. It's something else to think about.' She started to rise again.

'You should at least let your son worship with you, Mrs Grant.

My humble opinion. He desires spirituality. For what it's worth, he does not want to be a rancher like his father.'

'Look here, Jason. I don't actually worship God. We're more like friends, and I think we'd both prefer it if you stayed out of our relationship.' She was stalling with that, dealing with rage and shock simultaneously while trying to remember how to move her legs. 'In your humble opinion, what does my son want to do with his life?'

She thought, right then, she could be sick on this man's nasty carpet. For one thing, confronting the subject of her boy's future without Dalton felt like treason. But something else, something malignant now seemed to hover at the horizon. Jo could not have named it, but she felt it. Other Grant women might've told her that you cannot play in the light without acknowledging the dark, that the magic of her life which had become marvelously commonplace had an equally powerful flipside.

'He wants to travel for a start. He wants to develop his art abroad and have a fighting chance at making his mark. He wants a life – any life – of his own choosing that doesn't involve cattle. At least for a while. And he wants to try church.'

'Like I said, I'll think on it.'

Jo took the long way home. She had lost track of time. Lost her anger, lost her certainty in herself and all things, lost her intent. She had lost the ability to ask her mother's advice on how to run her household. Or she had very recently been propelled past the threshold where one mother's experience should rightly influence the ways and means of another. She felt as though, through some unforeseen turn of events, she had exhausted that precious bond, and this brought her to tears. She had never shared with Dalton the depth of her dependence on her mom, and so could not possibly make him understand her guilt and heartbreak at the loss of it. These feelings she considered childish and selfish, but the other things she would soon have to face were yet too fearsome. She felt weak at the moment and she wanted her mother.

Jo pulled the car over at a deserted gas station on the county line and sobbed until she trembled. She cried out and slapped the steering wheel and shouted, walleyed and impotent, at the windshield. She wanted it all out of her. Then she dried her eyes on the sleeve of her blouse and checked her face in the rearview.

It was late afternoon by the time she got home. Dalton would be coming in soon and he would be hungry. She heard music from the studio upstairs and knew her boy was working on something. She put on a load of clothes, took a shower, and set to cooking hamburgers because it was easy and quick to clean up. She was drained. Dalton walked through the back door at six sharp. Sander smelled the beef and was coming down the stairs about the same time. She was stacking burgers in a pyramid on the table and told them both to wash up before the patties got cold.

The kitchen sink had two basins but, of course, only one faucet. Jo was setting three places at the table and felt the floor shake a little. She looked up and saw them at the sink, both with soap on their hands, bumping each other with their hips, shoving back and forth. Laughing. Sander was taller than most men in town and broader, Dalton told her, than he was at that age. Dalton could still see the top of his head, though. The only time her boy looked like a kid anymore was with his daddy. Sander stomped on Dalton's booted foot and put his shoulder into the man to nudge him out of the way. Dalton chuckled, flicked a soapy hand at Sander's face and conceded the struggle in the name of hunger.

'You think you can take the old man?' he asked.

'Any day now,' Sander told him.

'You know where I live. When you think– Ouch!' Sander popped him on the rear with the dishtowel as he rinsed. 'When you think you're bad enough, bring it.'

Their smiles were contagious, but hers faded fast with the knowledge of what was coming. Jo didn't eat much. Sander cleared what few dishes there were and said he had a little more painting to finish before Jason came tomorrow. He excused himself. Dalton caught his wife staring vacantly at the baseboard.

'You wanna tell me what's wrong?'

'Tomorrow,' she said. 'I promise.'

'Where did you go today?'

'I just needed to get out.'

He put a hand on her shoulder and rubbed. 'Is that too hard?'

'No. It's perfect.' She closed her eyes.

'I hired your boy today. Eight hundred a month. Is he worth it?'

'I guess you'll find out. That feels so good,' she said, leaning her head into his hand.

'You're kinda pretty.'

'That's the sweetest thing any man has ever said to me.'

'I want to teach him to drive.' She didn't say anything. 'Is that okay?'

'If he's got a job, he's gonna need to. Right?'

'Yeah.'

'Be careful with him. I'm going to bed.'

'Is it that bad, Jo?'

'No, honey. It'll be okay. I'm just very tired.'

'Are we okay?'

She kissed his forehead as she stood. 'Yes.' And she went upstairs.

Jo had already eaten and had their breakfast ready when Sander and Dalton came down in the morning.

'I want you to see to your guys out there,' she told Dalton, 'get them doing whatever they need to be doing, and then I want you to come back inside. We're going to have a talk.'

'Alright.'

'You too, Sander. Get done what you need to and come to the living room.'

'How long's this gonna take, mamma? Jason will be here pretty soon.'

'No he won't. He's not coming today.'

Jo climbed onto the sofa and waited for them. She scanned the newspaper but couldn't concentrate. Thirty minutes later, in they came. Dalton sat beside her and Sander took the big chair, both of them wondering what had her riled.

Jo folded the paper and said, 'I went to town yesterday to do a little checking on Jason Markette.'

'I can't believe you did that, mamma.'

'Well, the sooner you believe I did it once, the easier it's gonna be on you when I do it the next time. Your friend has a history with drugs.'

'I already know that.'

'I know you do, and it's something you should've told me.'

'Do what?' Dalton wondered.

'Easy, honey.' She put a hand on his thigh. 'He said he hasn't taken them in a long time and I believe him. Sander, in a way it's good you two have talked about this. Saves me from preaching over something we both know I haven't a clue about.'

'You went to see him?'

'Yes I did. We talked about the time he spent in prison before he came here. Did he tell you about that?'

'Prison!' said Dalton. Jo squeezed his knee.

'Yes, ma'am. He said he got into some trouble. With the drugs,' Sander admitted.

'Prison!'

'Hush up a minute.' Then, to her son, 'Prison isn't "some trouble". Prison is prison. As long as you live in this house, you don't get to keep those secrets.'

'Mamma, I knew you wouldn't understand. He just made some mistakes, and he paid for them. It embarrasses me that you went and gave him the third degree behind my back.'

'It embarrassed me to have to, so we're in the same boat there. And you're right. I don't understand a person needing prison to teach him that lesson. I wouldn't have hired him if I'd known all this, but ...' She collected her thoughts and said, 'As long as we understand each other about secrets in my house, we don't need to discuss it further.'

Sander looked at his hands.

'Jason and I also talked about going to church,' said Jo.

'Is there something wrong with church?'

'Not at all. We never shared our views on it with you, and I can't for the life of me figure out why. We don't mind if you go to church. I'll even go with you if you want.'

'I want to go to Jason's.'

'That's fine. But go to others too. Whatever you end up placing your faith in, it shouldn't be only because Jason believes it.'

Dalton's thoughts were on the hill by the pond. Then, on his disdain for zealots, their clannish cruelty and herd-like mentality. What if his son became one of those? How would he tolerate that?

But he knew Jo was handling it the right way. If she spoke to God, then there was a God. Sander might stumble on his own way to commune with the guy, a way that had eluded generations of his people. He was plenty smart. Jo was saying something. Dalton felt her elbow in his ribs.

'Will you kindly participate?'

'Yes,' he said, 'I think church is a fine idea. You should see them all. See Jason's last.'

'Daddy, that's not fair.'

'Hell with fair. And so we're clear on this, drug use is not a mistake you're allowed.'

Jo was breathing a little easier. Drugs and religion were checked off her list for the time being and no major snags yet.

'And there's one more thing, a little more difficult to talk about. I don't know how much he's told you about girls, and I'm confessing to being a coward about the subject myself.'

'Sex? We talked about sex,' he told her.

'We're gonna talk about it some more.'

'Do we have to?'

'Afraid so. Did Jason tell you he's bisexual?'

Jo prepared herself for an outburst from Dalton's general direction, but none came. Silence.

'He is?' Sander asked. His face was difficult to read, changing rapidly as he shuffled through several possible feelings about this and, at the same time, wondered if it could be true.

'There's nothing wrong with him being what he is, either. But you are not that. It doesn't make you worldly or any more of a deep thinker to experiment with your sexuality. Do you know what I mean?'

'I think so.'

'You can come to me or your daddy anytime. Ask anything. And please, please, please use a condom until you get married. Will you do that?'

'Yes.'

Jo looked at Dalton. Her eyes went from pleading-wide to boring-narrow and he knew he better offer something else.

'Pregnancy is always serious, son. But with us, even more so. There are special issues because of our size and abortion some-times isn't possible, even early on.' He paused, studied the ceiling, then said, 'Do we need to talk about masturbation?'

'Dad, please.'

'Right. Like she said, come to me anytime.'

'So. Can I keep seeing Jason, or not?'

'Your daddy and I need to talk about it.'

As soon as he was up the stairs, Dalton said, 'What is there to talk about?'

'I don't want to keep him from Jason.' This discussion, Jo decided, was preferable to the one about Sander wanting a life that *doesn't involve cattle*. If he had truly said such a thing. Didn't sound like him. Either way, she thought as Dalton began his protest, Sander was a child. He would come to see their way of life much differently in a few years' time.

4

Sander's intellectual development nearly kept pace with his accelerated growth. It was the way with these men as far back as anyone knew. So, at eight years old, he recognized more wisdom in his parents' admonitions and advice than most young adults would. That is, after his anger subsided. As well, he no longer took for granted that he'd be allowed to keep seeing his tutor, his friend, if he didn't make certain concessions.

Therefore, Sander announced that he would begin his investigation into spirituality by asking Grandma Doris to take him to her church. They didn't go on a regular basis anymore, her and Frank. Sander knew this, but he suspected that was largely Frank's doing. He knew his mamma came by her close, if unorthodox relationship with God through her own mother, and that his grandma possessed an abiding and unshakeable faith. Doris still helped at the church when they needed her and she spoke with her preacher often.

His decision pleased Jo greatly and placated Dalton, who had always respected Doris's faith as a source of her peace and patience. Her brand of worship was a private matter, and he felt that she must likewise respect him, as she had never once evangelized. To Sander's surprise, when he brought it up at the next Sunday dinner, Frank said he would like to accompany them. Jo decided to let the three of them enjoy this experience without her. In truth, she felt nearly as uncomfortable inside a church as her husband would have – for different reasons, she imagined.

The following Sunday, Sander's grandparents picked him up at his house and they arrived at Mulberry Baptist just minutes before services commenced. Frank said that would minimize the obligatory hand pressing and general nosiness in the vestibule.

'They call it "fellowship", Frank told Sander. 'It's the only place I know of where somebody's right at ease asking how much money you make these days and are your hemorrhoids still giving you trouble. Because God's watching and they think you won't hit em.'

Sander, stretched out in the back seat trying not to wrinkle his pressed jeans, chuckled. Doris let Frank go on a bit, seeing that it eased her grandbaby.

They sat in the back of the sanctuary so Sander wouldn't block anyone's view and nobody would notice his boots jutting out into the aisle. The conservative atmosphere of his grandparents' church and almost dispassionate sermonizing of Dr Mullins was not remotely what Sander had expected, given the jubilance and communal spirit of the gatherings at First Unitarian Jason had described. Even the word Unitarian seemed more like something Sander would rather be associated with. As with all his endeavors, he took this task seriously, though, and willed the gates of his mind open.

The Reverend Dr Mullins spoke at great length on morality, forgiveness, and repenting. He used his Bible mainly for bibliographical notes and he had a habit of repeating himself while he thumbed the onion-skin pages for his next bookmark. These aims, Sander thought, need not have been decreed by God. After all, these are the ways civilized humans should act toward one another irrespective of their spiritual ties. He had expected to learn the Bible, to have the ancient scripture explained in terms relevant to his life, somewhat like Jason did, though more intensive. He didn't care much where in the book they started. He would catch up.

But that wasn't what this service was about. Sander felt underdressed and disrespectful in his expectations. Still, did the rest of the congregation really need to hear this kind of stuff week in and week out, lest they forget? At least nobody stared at him. As he kept wondering if this was what it was like in here every Sunday, Sander found himself staring– at all the unmoving hair in front of him, parts and curls glued in place. He pondered the sheer mass of hairspray in the room and knew he was going to have to buy his own Bible and begin reading it before he tried this again. With that determination, he fell asleep to the musty smell of the hymnals.

He awoke to the amplified tinkling of a piano behind the pulpit. It was a slow, simple composition and seemed to be going nowhere. As he stifled a yawn, a woman from the choir began to sing. Sander couldn't see her, but she had the most beautifully melodic southern twang, like a bell with bending notes.

> Softly and tenderly Jesus is calling,
> calling for you and for me;
> see, on the portals he's waiting and watching,
> watching for you and for me.

Sander concentrated on the refrain, *'come home, come home ...'* What a song, that sweet beckoning, and what a voice. This, he thought, this is what they should sing to children at night. Just like she's doing it. He craned his neck to find the owner of that voice, but Dr Mullins remained at the microphone and began his own calling.

In a hypnotic baritone, the preacher urged, 'Come to the Lord, sinner come. He's waiting for you. Right here, right now. Commit your life to Jesus before the congregation. Don't keep Him waiting.'

Though Mullins gazed across many sets of eyes as he did this, Sander thought the Reverend Doctor might have tarried on his face a bit longer. There was a benign pressure to the summons, but powerful, a current running beneath the ritual of the thing. Here was something new. Did this happen every Sunday? Sander felt an odd tug in his chest, pulling him toward the stage. Was there some preparation for this that he had missed? Others in the congregation seemed to be rounding up their belongings, waking their children and preparing to leave.

He leaned over to Doris. 'Is he talking to me, grandma?' Because, nobody else was going up there. Maybe they already had.

Before Doris could answer, an elderly deacon standing against the back wall stepped forward and put his hand on Sander's shoulder and it startled him.

'Yes, son,' said the deacon. '*He's* waiting for you, too.'

The family in front of Sander heard, turned and smiled.

Frank was incensed. He brushed the man's hand off his grandson.

'Can you not give the boy room to breathe, Cecil? It's like you're peddling timeshares or something.' Frank was genetically incapable of whispering. Cecil retreated and Frank mumbled, 'Creep up on a person like that. Damn.'

Now the folks from several pews up were turned and looking

back. They were not smiling. The song played on and more deacons appeared in the aisles with collection plates.

'Come on,' said Doris, patting Sander's thigh. 'Time to go.'

Frank glared at Cecil as they passed and Doris dropped a ten-dollar bill in the slotted box near the door.

Over the following weeks, it was much the same, absent Frank and Doris. Sometimes Sander asked his mother along, most times not. As he had done in school, he learned to ignore the gawking. He became accustomed to the intrusive questions, the visitor cards, prayer requests, and the gentle but persistent pressure to hurry up and join most of the churches he entered. He was astonished once when a pastor asked all the newcomers to stand before the service began so that the members might notice them and make them feel welcome. Sander constituted 'all the newcomers.' Standing there while four hundred seated people eyeballed him with impunity, he certainly felt like one of the group. Nevertheless, he remained undaunted. Dutifully, he went on to visit The Latter Day Saints, several different Methodist and Presbyterian services, The Church of Christ, Pentecostals, and something called The Seventh Day Adventists – which he missed on his first attempt, assuming they held service on Sundays like the rest. He carried ten dollars with him to each sermon and placed it in the tray. This he did out of respect.

He rounded off his list with the Lutherans, because he loved the music of Bach and figured the famously devout Lutheran might have been pretty smart. Finally, he made his way to the one Catholic church in town just to see what Martin Luther found so objectionable. It was hard to tell. Anyway, these last two were far and away his favorites, simply for the fact that, though they too were friendly, he sensed in every Lutheran and Catholic a private confidence in why they were there. Moreover, they really didn't seem to care what had brought Sander among them.

And that represented every faith and denomination in Dixon, except Jason's.

After his first lackluster experience at Mulberry Baptist, he had gone straight out and bought himself a Bible. Sander quizzed the woman at New Life Bible Book Store regarding the four versions they offered until she was ready to give him one of each to see him gone. He settled on the King James Version, acknowledging the caveat that it was only King James's version. The woman at the store didn't put it like that. She said that Hebrew was a tough language to translate into English because many of the Old Testament words had multiple meanings. Some of the other Biblical versions left those words in Hebrew. Unless you wanted to translate them on your own, the KJV was your best bet.

That night, Sander took a pencil and notepad to his room and started on page 1. He got all the way to page 9 before finding Genesis chapter 6, verse 4:

> There were giants in the earth in those days; and also after
> that, when the sons of God came in unto the daughters
> of men, and they bare children to them, the same became
> mighty men which were of old, men of renown.

He didn't leap up to share this with anyone, suddenly feeling stupid, feeling that all his life people had known this was written here and, for whatever reason, they didn't feel the need to tell him. He stared at the wall in his bedroom for the remainder of the night, not moving, not reading further, only vacillating between frustration, embarrassment, and excitement. When the sun rose, he determined that he would need more notepads, and much more time to read. The time to talk to someone about what he discovered in these pages – and there were so many pages – would come when he had digested the work in full. He figured this would take six months, minimum. It wasn't an easy read.

When his mother asked about his experiences in the various churches, Sander freely gave his insight. Jo passed some of this along to Dalton and it pleased him. His son wasn't impressed with what he saw. That much was obvious. His determination would wane, Dalton felt sure. Jo anticipated that day too, but appended a private hope to her anticipation that Sander would then come to her and ask for another way to know God. She hoped that would take at least another few weeks, because he might also ask her to help him reconcile why he could talk to his dead grandfather but could not hear God, as she did. Jo would need an answer for that and she had yet to find one.

The guys had taken their first trip to the hill by the pond somewhere around his two weeks of trial Presbyterianism. Jo couldn't remember. They were all running together. At any rate, Dalton handled it much the same as his own father had. Will confessed that he had no idea how to broach the subject of speaking with the dead, and Dalton hadn't any brainstorms on it either. So, that day, he just told Sander they were going for a walk. He said he had something of a surprise to show the boy as they neared the pond, and then he wasted no time.

They sat beneath the oak and Dalton said, 'Daddy?'

This took Sander off guard, but not as much as when Will replied, 'Hey, boy.' Then, 'Hello, Sander.'

Sander sprang to his feet. 'Oh shit.'

'It's alright, son. Please,' Dalton said. He patted the grass. 'It's only your grandfather.'

'Only?' said Will. He was chuckling, seeing Sander ready to take flight and remembering the experience when he was a kid. 'Boo,' he said. The land rumbled.

'Stop it, daddy,' Dalton told him. 'Hang on just a minute.'

'It's coming out of there,' Sander said, pointing at the tree roots. 'I can feel it.'

'We buried him here. Remember? I told you that. We're all buried here.' Dalton searched his son's eyes.

'Is he– Are they alive in there?'

'No. They're not.'

Will piped up, 'Don't talk about me like I'm not here.' His voice was sober and commanding now. 'Sander, sit down.'

After a moment, Sander sat. He leaned his head toward the ground and shouted, 'How many of you are down there?'

'Quit hollering at the grass. You'll scare the cattle,' said Will. 'There's four of us. We all hear you but you can only hear me. I'm the only one with anything useful to say, anyway and–' He broke off, then continued, laughing, 'My pop's name is Jedediah. He says hello. Gramps is Bartholomew, says the fence looks shoddy on the northeast corner. And Augustus is your great-great-great-grandfather. He wants me to tell you you're a good looking kid, as big as him at nine years old.' When Sander didn't say anything, Will said, 'Augustus was forty stone on his twelfth birthday. Looks like you're gonna be a stout one.'

Dalton watched his son closely. They shared a glance and he nodded to Sander.

'I know it's a lot to take in,' said Dalton.

'It aint a trick?' his son asked.

'It aint an it,' Will said. 'It's me. You didn't get this far in life without realizing that you're a tad different than everybody else. This is just another one of those differences. Doesn't make you weird, boy. Makes you special.'

'Makes me nauseous,' Sander said.

'Yeah,' said Dalton. 'That goes away.'

'Can you,' Sander stuttered, 'talk to others like us that aren't buried here?'

'We can. Don't know many of them all that well. There's three in south Texas with Augustus's father, and one up in –' He stopped himself. 'And lots of us across the ocean that we don't strictly get along with. We've been on our own for a while now, Sander. The clans split and sort of scattered to the wind. It was better that way, but we lost touch with one another and now they're hard to find.' Will spoke to Dalton. 'Son, why don't you let us get to know one another? He's alright now.'

Dalton hesitated, then asked his father, 'Remember what we talked about?'

Will sighed. 'I got it.'

Dalton turned to Sander, 'You okay?'

'I guess. Where you going?'

'I'll meet you back at the house. Don't be late for dinner.'

Sander watched his daddy walking away. A thought occurred to him and he shouted, 'Does mamma know about this?'

Dalton didn't turn. And despite his warnings about being late, Sander would've stayed there all night, but his ancestors were in unanimous agreement that pissing off Jo was a bad start to their relationship. There would be time, Will assured Sander, to say everything that needed saying. He could come back anytime he wanted. And this he did, much more often than his father. Dalton knew the old men would start to grate on him after a while and the visits would become less frequent. Until then, he rejoiced in Sander's closeness to his kin, to his past. Or at least that past he had permitted his own father to share. Since his boy had accepted and eventually welcomed this aspect of their difference, as Will put it, any zealous church-goers wanting Sander's trust hereafter would have to be supremely open-minded. That, in Dalton's mind, pretty well narrowed the field to zero.

Meanwhile, Sander's art lessons continued. Jason only came for scheduled tutoring sessions, which were shortened considerably and moved to Tuesday and Friday nights. As he was not done with his forays into the town's other sundry denominations, Sander allowed no talk of spirituality when Jason came, even if said spirituality applied to the subject of art itself. Jason understood.

Weeks became months and a new normalcy settled in on the ranch. Sander didn't talk as much, and he moved more deliberately about his tasks in the fields, like he had something pressing to do afterward. His daddy would catch him in moments of contemplation, moments the boy had previously spent chattering on about the purpose of art, or idly soaping a saddle in the gloaming before supper. Now he sometimes stood motionless with a look on his face like he was committing an idea to memory for lack of a pencil to jot it down. None of this affected his work, though. If anything, it made him more efficient.

After a time, Dalton wondered how much more Jason could possibly have to teach Sander. It wasn't the cost of the lessons. With Sander's help, business was flourishing, herd numbers stabilized and slowly increased. It was, as Jason himself would admit, that Sander's paintings were now outstanding by any yardstick. Dalton was thankful that his son had not yet begun painting nudes, but he had to wonder how Jason imparted the knowledge – if that's where it came from – of the human form which allowed Sander to so accurately depict people in his work. He knew his boy would be showing his work soon, and that would bring with it a whole new set of difficulties. He could already envision the media scuttlebutt surrounding the painting kid-giant. Sander would soon pass seven feet tall. Both his parents worried that his stature might eclipse his talent. Dalton privately worried that Jason might be hanging around to soak up some of that attention for himself, to take credit for Sander's gift.

Knowing what he did about the artist, Dalton was never again able to stay for a long stretch in the house while Jason was there. No doubt Jason thought it was an incurable case of homophobia, since Sander had told him of the family discussion they had that day in the living room. If Jason thought that, he was wrong. The differences between people were things Dalton and all his kin were very tolerant of, for obvious reasons. And Dalton knew that mistakes were valuable teaching tools. Many a time he had told Sander this, way before Jason Markette arrived. Though he failed to qualify that lesson. Didn't, back then, feel any need to. This omission troubled him now.

Dalton drew a hard line between mistakes made in an effort to accomplish something, and mistakes made because you're bored and stupid and feel like you can get away with whatever in hell you want. In short, to Dalton's mind, Jason acted as though these latter-type blunders afforded him the same insight as the former. Sander had a deep well of understanding in him, though, which gave him a keen eye for bullshit. With no other options regarding the subject of Jason, Dalton was banking on this understanding to bring his son through.

In the fields, Sander expected to be treated as any other ranch hand. His patience grew, while his drive and eagerness to learn remained undiminished. He soaked up his daddy's knowledge like a sponge, and took more advice from Will and his ancestors than Dalton would tolerate. The Grant intuition for livestock soon ripened in him and he became an indispensable aid to the operation.

Dalton got around to calling Elgin Breeding Service early that fall. They agreed, for a fee, to come out and design, then supervise the construction of a small semen collection and storage facility on Grant land. Collection did not present so much a problem for Dalton as it did with others. Not only could Dalton keep the bulls calm in the chutes, he could pick them up and place them there. The cost of storage, however, with the requisite freezers, back-up generators, and sterile environment, was substantial.

Dalton and Sander took the plans from Elgin and built the facility themselves. They spent every dollar they could squeeze out of the books, sold the herd back down to two hundred and seventy head, then set about building the business up once more. It fell to Sander to learn how to run the storage facility by himself. So he had a full time job by his ninth birthday, and a full load of academic courses five days a week.

School let out for the year and this freed up much more time for Sander, but there never seemed quite enough. Summer nights were for reading next year's text books, then his Bible, which often sent him in search of more reading material as he doggedly chased down every locatable discourse on the Moabites, the Emims, the Anakims, Zamzummims and every other strange moniker his King James had for big people. He devoured books of all feather now, except other versions of the Bible itself. This version alone was sufficient to have him on a first-name basis with Marjorie Porter at the library reference desk. Much of the gas burned in the ranch pickup was due to Sander's frequent visits to Dixon's Barrett Memorial Library. He had already exhausted the one at the school.

Early mornings were for painting, then came work through the afternoon, and many evenings, schedule permitting, he spent on the hill by the pond. Sander privately considered that time as his most valuable schooling. History in its own voice, something he felt his daddy neglected to take full advantage of. Then it was back to reading by lamplight. He set a clock in his studio, against vehement protest from Jason, and minutes after the alarm went off every morning, Dalton would look up and see Sander striding across the pasture, digging paint from his fingernails with his pocket knife and donning his own buckskin gloves. His life had become, of necessity, highly regimented. He slept less than anyone in the house, sometimes only an hour a night.

Jo saw all of this, but fought the urge to nag him about it. Sander needed to figure out for himself what was important enough to strive for and what sacrifices must be offered to achieve it. Neither were thoughts such as that beyond her son. As ever, he was learning. She didn't know how much he was learning.

5

Jason understood the demands on Sander's time. He just didn't agree with the priority system in place. Nothing to be done about that. The boy was being pulled in half a dozen different directions and getting between him and his family wouldn't serve any good purpose. Sander had promised that he would visit First Unitarian only after he visited the other churches on his list. Jason didn't like that, either, but likewise kept his mouth shut. He, too, had faith in Sander's intelligence and he could tell the boy was frustrated with his religious experiences to date.

School was well underway again and there remained scant wiggle room in Sander's hectic schedule. Thanksgiving was upon them before anyone around the house could entertain three consecutive thoughts without returning to the financial status of Grant Beef. Things were tight, but in the best possible way. They had a plan, of which Sander was no small part, and they were digging out as fast as their cattle could breed. While the herd numbers were low, Dalton made ends meet selling hay and, now that the semen operation was up and running smoothly, Sander was able to put in enough hours at other ranch duties that Dalton could lay off two field hands. Jo even found that she had a knack for running the New Holland tractor and could handle most of its attachments. They were making it work. Pride eclipsed exhaustion for the most part.

It was mid-December when Sander informed Jason that he would attend First Unitarian the following Sunday. He wanted to make sure it would be a regular service and not a Christmas pageant or something.

Jason laughed. 'I guess you haven't seen our place, huh? Sander, we don't have enough people for a respectable Christmas pageant. Anyway, some of us observe Christmas and Easter, others observe the solstices. A few, like me, thank the Lord for a day off work here and there and try to avoid the shopping traffic. So, yes, this week would be a fine one to visit.'

Sander didn't tell his parents where he was going that morning until he asked for the truck keys. He had more than lived up to his end of the bargain and felt there shouldn't be any discussion about it. There wasn't, but it had nothing to do with any bargain. Jo and Dalton no longer considered that their boy was in danger of making rash decisions regarding religion or anything else. The pendulum had swung the other way. Parents have to worry about something, though, and now they were concerned that his childhood, such as a Grant boy has, was being apportioned and consumed, forequarters by the ranch and hindmost by his studies. He had to get away from it all for a while. If Jason's church was the enticement he needed, so be it. They saw their son toting around those books on Pythagoras and Voltaire, so what harm could some left-wing tambourine-bangers do?

Sander knew the area, but Jason was right, he'd never paid any attention to their church in driving by it. There was no sign. First

Unitarian met in a two-story clapboard house in a residential neighborhood on Eden Drive, just inside the Dixon city limits. Much of the yard was graveled for parking. It was an old place, but well-kept. The bottom-story had been gutted, except for the kitchen and bathroom, and remodeled as a meeting hall. Roger Carlson lived upstairs. It was as nice inside as many of the brick churches on the highway, only much smaller. The pews might've held thirty before things got tight and elbows started knocking. Not a problem, however, as Sander soon learned that Roger's flock numbered but twenty-two.

Jason introduced Sander to most of them, and it seemed each had some claim on the improvements or operation of the place.

'Sander, this is Mike, our master carpenter. George and Laura help him. Laura is also a fine bookkeeper.' Next was, 'Joyce, she cooks for us on Wednesdays.' And, 'Alfonse put this roof on – what? – last year.' Then, 'Neil and Carla Rae are our painters.' And on it went.

Sander mumbled, 'No free rides here.'

'Like a real hippie commune,' said Randall, the resident electrician. Sander didn't think anyone was close enough to hear. 'I know. But that's not really the point. Nobody has to work. Some can't, so they help with the bills. We do what we do because nobody else is gonna do it and because it's ours.'

'Not God's?' Sander asked.

'Heck would God want this place for? We're the ones need the heater to work and the toilet to flush. I'm not saying God couldn't pitch in if He felt like it. We just figured He's got a few other things to do, so we try to keep it nice for when He visits.'

Sander felt comfortable, like he was calling on a group of Jason's friends. He was not the center of attention or even the subject of conversation. Most of the men wore jeans like him. They might've been congregated down at the Feed & Seed, absent the smell of nitrogen fertilizer and cages of Banty pullets. There were people laughing loudly about something in that corner over there, and somebody was brewing coffee in the kitchen. Nobody stared at him. Nobody whispered. There were no visitor cards, no slotted box for his ten-dollar bill.

'It's almost time,' said Jason. 'Why don't we have a seat?'

They did, and Sander noticed the back pew had been moved, giving it twice the leg room of the rest.

Roger Carlson came down the stairs in a huff, apologizing profusely for running late as he made his way past the congregation to the front of the room. There was neither a microphone nor a podium up there. Just a blackboard, about four feet square and two-sided, where it could be flipped on its axis. Roger was a thoroughly average-looking man of fifty-something, sandy hair and slightly ruddy complexion. He was the kind of person who wouldn't draw attention, dressed today in a pair of cotton pants and a tweed sport coat that had seen some wear.

Once in front of them, Roger grinned and said, 'Good morning.' He glanced to the back and added, 'Welcome, Sander.' That was it. Nobody looked around. Roger took a piece of chalk from his pocket, turned to the blackboard and wrote:

Is God Perfect?

Facing them, he asked, 'Well?' and waited. 'Come on, now. That's gotta inspire some knee-jerk reactions.'

'Perfect in what way?' asked a young man in the front, sensing a loaded question.

'Oh, don't go philosophical on me this early in the morning, Andrew.' A few people snickered. 'You know what I mean.'

'Yes, to me He is,' said Neil the painter.

Roger nodded. 'Good answer. Safe, but good.'

'I don't think so,' said Alfonse. 'I mean, I don't think perfect is the word.'

'Why?' Roger asked.

'Because He repented,' said the roofer, and Sander immediately knew where he was going with this. 'He says so, right off the bat.'

Roger's smile returned. 'Somebody's been reading Genesis. I like that. "And it repented the Lord that he had made man on the earth, and it grieved him at his heart." That's chapter 6, yall.'

He shot an involuntary glance at Sander, realizing that a mere two inches above that verse is where Moses first writes of giants. Roger heard pages turning and wanted to steer them forward from that passage and so said, 'Let's circle back to that – whether "it repented the Lord" really means the Lord repented. Remind me later, Alfonse, alright?' Alfonse nodded. 'For now, let's jump ahead to the flood, chapter 7, starting at verse 21, I think.' Roger waited for them to find the page.

'It would seem that God's making a point, wouldn't it? I mean, He's wiping us out, and it's not mentioned in passing. Three whole verses begin, respectively, "And all flesh *died* that moved upon the earth ..." then "All in whose nostrils was the breath of life ..." so on and so forth ... "*died*" and one more time, for good measure, "And every living substance was *destroyed* ..."' He paused. 'Is Moses trying to tell us something here?' Roger turned to the board and wrote:

Man – mistake?

'But then, why not have Noah load the animals on the boat, nail the door shut and cast that sucker off? Why save a few of us? That sounds like me when I was trying to give up smoking. I'd toss out every Chesterfield in the house. Get thee rid of those nasty cancer sticks and be quit of it forevermore! Except that pack in the nightstand.' Sander heard guffaws in agreement, saw heads nodding. Roger shrugged.

For some reason, this folksy, proletariat approach to the subject matter of divine wrath struck Sander as flippant. True, Roger was reaching his people and Sander hadn't witnessed a more natural teacher. Regardless, he felt like challenging the man. All of the preachers, pastors, reverends, rectors, and priests he'd seen had earmarked passages relevant to the day's message. Some, like Roger, had even gone to the trouble of memorizing a few verses. That only meant they did a little homework last night. It evidenced no understanding.

Roger was saying, '... so mankind might not actually be a mistake in God's eyes. You think? Maybe there were just some bad ones in the bunch?'

This guy never gives any answers, Sander thought, and he boomed, 'Maybe He just killed the ones He really hated.' He didn't expect his voice would carry quite so well in the little space. It startled several people, Jason seemed to draw away from his side, and Sander was sorry for that. He continued, more softly, with a question of his own. 'Does a perfect being hate?'

'No, Sander. I would say not.' Roger pointed his chalk at Joyce the cook, who sat on the first row. 'You've got better eyes than me, hon. Could you read for us from Malachi?' Sander noticed then that, bad eyes notwithstanding, Roger carried no Bible.

Joyce found Malachi and asked, 'Which chapter?'

'Just start from the beginning, please.'

'"The burden of the word of the Lord to Israel by Malachi,"' read Joyce. '"I have loved you, saith the Lord. Yet ye say, Wherein has thou loved us? Was not Esau Jacob's brother? saith the Lord: yet I loved Jacob, And I hated–"' She broke off and all was quiet save a dripping faucet in the kitchen. Which one of them was the plumber, again?

'Is that what you're talking about, Sander?'

'That's one spot.'

'Yeah,' Roger nodded, 'a personal favorite. Keep reading, Joyce.'

'"And I hated Esau, and laid his mountains and his heritage waste for the dragons of the wilderness."'

'Okay. Thank you.' Roger turned to the board and wrote:

> God hates

The declarative sentence pleased Sander.

'Not only does He hate,' Roger said, 'but, according to the following verses, He carries on with His indignation forever. An unforgiving, divine hatred. Oh, and God says there are dragons. Not something we've ever discussed before. By show of hands, who thinks there were dragons back then?' Roger let that dangle before them and nobody dared touch it. 'Then again, how much of the Bible did God actually write?'

'I can't find any of it written by God,' said Sander.

'Well,' said Roger, tapping 'God hates' on the blackboard, 'we know Malachi wrote that part. His byline is right up top. So it starts out as hearsay and we cannot be sure how it's been changed, edited, and pieced together since.' He took Joyce's Bible and held it up. 'For the purpose of knowing God, though, is this all we're given?'

'The world and all that's in it,' somebody said. Sander couldn't tell who.

'Now we're talking.' Roger scrawled those words on his blackboard and underlined them. 'So let's ask ourselves how perfect a place this is, and extrapolate from there something about the being who made it. Why don't we start with childhood cancer and nuclear weapons? They're as good as dragons and everlasting hatred, and we know for sure they exist. But,' he said, 'before we go too far down that road, I want to caution you; God doesn't appreciate armchair criticism. Unless you know of someone who could've done it better.'

On the board, he wrote:

War Plague Crime Oppression

He said, 'There's a sizeable part of our world. And that's either downright meanness, or somebody messed up somewhere.'

Confusion befell the congregation and Roger had them. Now, unlike when they walked in here, they actually required some answers in order to carry on. None of these people, Sander thought, would leave here now if the building were ablaze. Their faith was laid bare.

Roger told them, 'It's the first thing God admits to us, the fallibility of omnipotence. He tells us that omnipotent, omniscient, and ubiquitous aren't synonymous. They're not even distant cousins. He tells us this to prepare us for what's left to do – what we have to deal with.' He counted them off on three fingers, 'All-powerful, all-knowing, and ever-present. That would be quite a feat, the ultimate hat trick. But two out of three aint bad. Once upon a time, the Greeks knew this about their Gods, that mistakes were sometimes made. And they revered and worshiped them all nonetheless.

Somewhere along the line, we decided that wasn't good enough. We had to make our God into something He never claimed to be – perfect.' He held the Bible up once more, 'We just haven't expunged all the evidence to the contrary. Give us time. Meanwhile, we knew right off, if God was to be perfect, we had to have somebody else to blame for all this other inconvenient stuff. Who could we pin it on?' Roger took a long look at the blackboard and scratched his chin with the leather spine of Joyce's King James. 'And if we pin it on somebody else, would he not be of God's hand as well?' Turning to his congregation, 'Gets tough when we start playing with the facts, don't it?'

He extended Joyce her Bible and she checked it for injury while he switched gears and continued.

'Which brings me to the second thing God wants us to know. He didn't write that book. Didn't even endorse it. But much of it, even in its corrupted form, is gospel. And – listen carefully to this – those parts which are not strictly accurate can tell us just as much as credible history. If we know the difference. So let's talk about how we parse this thing for truth, that we might see what's offered by the rest.'

Sander checked his watch when the lecture was done. He would not call this a sermon because that term demeaned it. It had lasted nearly two hours. Jason said he and some of the congregation were staying to cook a meal, but Sander told him there was work at the ranch that he needed to get done.

'I'll call you later,' said Jason, and made his way to the kitchen as Sander left.

Roger caught Sander at his truck in the lawn. 'Not hungry?' he asked.

'I'm always hungry, but my mother will have something ready and I've got to get back.'

'Did you enjoy the meeting?'

'It was different. Thanks for scooting the pew back for me.'

'We didn't scoot anything. It was built that way, bolted to the floor like the rest. Tell me something. When did you discover that your people were in the Bible?'

This shocked Sander and he fought not to show it. 'I'm not sure it's talking about my people.'

'I think you've got more than a passing suspicion. When did you read it?'

'I started a few months ago. Finished recently. One thing I am suspicious about, though. Is it God who wants us to know He had nothing to do with the Bible, or is it you?'

Roger nodded and looked at his scuffed loafers. 'I didn't say He had nothing to do with it, but I'm not positive He was, let's say, enthusiastic about today's talk. Overall.'

'Why didn't you ask Him?'

'It's easier to apologize. He'll stop me if I go too far.'

'Well, since God didn't write the stuff, and we've now discovered it's inaccurate, I'm not going to spend much time searching for any of my relatives in there.'

'Makes good sense. Until you ask yourself what kind of hereditary trait might persist for hundreds of years, never skipping a generation. How dominant would that gene need to be?' Roger seemed to ponder his own question for a few seconds. Then he turned and saw several members of the congregation standing on the porch, looking at them. 'You should talk to someone about what you've read, someone who's studied the text at length. Knowledge always helps and never hurts, though it may be painful.'

'Talk to you, you mean.'

'I hold a Doctor of Theology from Harvard. Various degrees in history, archeology, yada-yada. My resume, in short. Makes me sound like a pompous ass, I know. I'd be honored to help you, but there's a lot of smart people out there. Just make sure whomever you speak to has what you're looking for, right? And not some superstitious bullshit. Have a good afternoon, Sander. Thanks for stopping by.'

'You too.' It was all Sander could think to say.

As he started the truck, Roger trotted back over. What now, thought Sander. He didn't know how much more he could process today. He rolled down his window.

'Almost forgot.' Roger handed him an envelope from his coat pocket. 'I've been saving this for you. Give it a read when you get some time. And I hope it goes without saying that your entire family is welcome here.'

'Thanks.'

Sander tucked the envelope into his back pocket without a thought. On the drive home, he concentrated on finding one thing Roger Carlson had said that he disagreed with. It would be much easier to distrust him, to doubt him, to dislike him, at least a little. He parked in front of the gate back home. Lunch was ready and on the table. He ate with his parents and waited for the questions. When none came, he excused himself and went upstairs to change into his work clothes.

Folding his pressed jeans, he found the envelope tucked into the back pocket and sat on his bed to open it. There was a single word on the outside: Nephilim. Inside was a Xerox copy of a newspaper article. It was old, blurry in places, and Sander had to squint to read.

New Castle News

Monday September 15, 1913
Vera Townsman Unearths a Giant Frame of
Murdered Cattleman in Oklahoma

BARTLESVILLE: – Early days in what was formerly
Indian Territory are being recalled by the discovery of the
skeleton of a man unearthed at Vera, this county, a few
days ago, not to mention many relics such as revolvers,
parts of rifles used years ago, that are also being found.
For, a quarter of a century ago on this side of the state,
especially in Washington County, scores of crimes were
committed and many a man was sent to his grave, buried
in the wilderness and one more life was added to the
long list of tragedies that gave Indian Territory a national
reputation as the home of bad men. Civilization, though,
has changed conditions and no longer do 'bad men' travel
over the prairies unmolested.

Just the other day a Vera resident was digging a
foundation for a house. Three feet beneath the surface he
found the skeleton of a man. The bones indicated that the
victim of a knife or a revolver was a large man. Oldtimers
in Vera recalled that about a quarter of a century ago a
cattleman suddenly disappeared. It was thought he had
gone west, although he had made no provisions for his
property and had never indicated he intended leaving.
Now it is believed the human skeleton just found was
that of the cattleman who disappeared a quarter of a
century ago.

At the bottom, Roger had written, 'Do you know who that cattleman
was?' Sander stared at it for a moment. There was no name in the
article, so of course he didn't know who it was. Nor did he know
anyone named Nephilim. He put the paper back in the envelope,
the envelope in his Bible and shoved it under his bed. He knew
there was hard work outside that could wait no longer.

Beyond the gate, Dalton stood by the bay door at the barn, gloves in hand.

'I thought you'd already have the tractor out there,' said Sander. 'Is it broke?'

'It aint broke. I'm waiting on Javier. Said he'd be here after lunch. I thought we'd let him drive while you and I load together. Some quality time, I think is what they call it.'

Dalton looked Sander up and down. Lately, the worry and the work and the unforgiving minute had robbed him of a long overdue appraisal of his boy. Sander hadn't shaved this morning, that's the first thing he noticed. The stubble on his brick of a jaw had a red tint to it, but not so much that it didn't match his brown hair. Dalton was slouching against the barn, but he estimated that if he stood erect – and he resisted the urge to do so – his head wouldn't top Sander's but a few inches. His son would be ten feet tall in a year. Their hands were the same size. Sander's feet were already bigger. His shoulders wider. He needed some meat on his arms and back, but he was likely within a hundred pounds of Dalton's weight.

'What did the preacher man have to say?'

Sander shook his head. 'Said little people were a bad idea.'

They laughed.

'Well,' said his daddy, 'I guess you can't get everything right.'

'Said that, too.'

'I heard you and Jason–' He started again, 'I wasn't snooping on you. Walking by in the hall I heard you and Jason talking about selling some of your work.'

'Yeah. He thinks it's time.'

'You?'

'I'm not sure yet. Jason says he knows of buyers for my style and he'll make the introductions. Better than having to do a show and all.'

'It would be,' Dalton agreed, 'but might not get you the exposure, if that's what you're looking for.'

'Not so much. If I could just bring in a little money, that's all I'm after. Clear out my studio a bit and help out with the bills. Besides, if I were to show up at a gallery over in Tyler or Dallas, the whole thing would be about me. A freak show. Better that the art goes its own way without me, is what I mean.'

'Don't call us freaks, boy.'

'I didn't. They would.'

'Hell with them. But,' said Dalton, 'there aint no way you're gonna keep yourself a secret. They're gonna come looking.'

'I guess they will. It'll pass. And like I said, it's money. Jason says I should price my bigger pieces in the five-hundred dollar range.'

'I'm no judge of art, but I've got eyes. From what I've seen, Jason's on the low side. You're good. Your stuff is special and I'm proud of you.'

'Thanks, dad.'

'And if I see one dollar of that money paying ranch bills, I'll whip you till you can't sit down. That's your money and I want you to save it, you hear?'

Nothing.

'You hear?'

'Yes, sir.'

'Yonder comes Javier. Let's throw some hay.'

Dalton stood and gave Sander a shove. The boy didn't budge.

'Keep up long as you can,' Sander said, 'but when you get winded, go ahead and sit down. I don't want you to hurt yourself.'

'Right.'

They were putting on their gloves as the Mexican ranch hand walked up between them. When Dalton fished the tractor key from his pocket and dropped it in his hand, Javier looked like a beggar kid on the streets of a border town. The flatbed trailer was already hitched to the New Holland and Javier wasted no time in pulling it around the barn and heading east to the rows of bales. Father and son trotted over and jumped on the trailer for the ride.

The tractor stopped at the south corner of the hayfield. Javier idled the engine. Dalton surveyed the two hundred acres. Geometric rows of round bales, spaced ninety feet apart. This was hay they knew they would sell. The last growing season had been a short one and their meager budget allowance for fertilizer of late meant the crude protein content wasn't nearly what Grant stock required. Which also meant these bales were light, about five hundred pounds apiece.

'Wasting daylight,' Dalton said.

In the past, Sander had always been the catcher. He stayed on the trailer, situating each new bale against the last as Dalton heaved them up, three high.

Today, he said, 'Take it easy. Let me throw some.'

'Get after it,' his daddy told him as he stood on the flatbed and motioned Javier ahead.

The weight of the first few caught Sander by surprise and Dalton saw it. He didn't offer any help, only motioned for Javier to slow a bit off the pace they were accustomed to moving. By the end of the first row, Sander had figured out how to use his legs to get under the bales, then rotate his trunk to let the weight carry itself from his arms. Sort of bellying the bales over.

Problem was, in the middle of the second row, he now had to throw the things on top of the first layer, another five feet up, at least. He could feel his heartbeat all the way down in his thighs and it was increasingly difficult to catch his breath between bales. He began to wonder if he was doing it much faster than a little tractor with a hay spike.

Dalton stood atop the hay, feet spread for balance, looking like the Colossus of Rhodes waiting for something to do. Sander no longer believed he had the vaguest notion of his father's strength. Even his gloves were drenched with sweat. If he stopped to suck wind, hands on his knees, he had to run to catch the tractor again. Still Dalton made no move to assist, didn't bend to grab the netting of a single bale. He wanted to see if Sander would quit.

When the second layer was solid, Dalton hollered for Javier to stop. He hopped off the trailer and patted Sander on the back.

'If you're not all spent, climb on up there and let me show you something.'

Sander hadn't the breath to respond. He made his way up and the tractor started again, in second gear. Dalton trotted alongside, covering the distance between bales in long strides. His son didn't see the first one leave the ground, but he heard it – *vooof* – and got his feet under him just before it hit him in the chest. Javier was grinning up there as the tractor seat bounced on its springs.

'I wish one of us could sing,' shouted Dalton.

Vooof.

'It would help. You know, the rhythm of it and all. Don't you think?'

Vooof.

Sander was watching more closely now. Dalton paid no attention to the netting as a handhold. Instead, he drove his fists into the sides of the bales, latching onto them like a two-pronged logging grapple, then swinging them skyward in one fluid motion, all while moving forward. When the third layer was done, he climbed up with his son and they rode to the pole barn in silence. They would unload, ride back, and do it again until dark, as always. If they were to finish this field today, though, Sander knew he had to stay on the trailer.

6

Sander slowed his breakneck progression through school once he hit eighth grade. There were a number of reasons. He knew he wouldn't be going to college. Had no desire to, so what was the hurry? He was beginning to doubt he'd stick it out until graduation at Dixon High. The classes grew more boring every year, the facilities more uncomfortable no matter how they tried to accommodate his size; his home and the lumber yard being the only places he could stand erect indoors. He figured tenth grade would just about do it for him. And he liked working with his daddy full time in the summer without worrying about what text he should be reading to make sure he didn't miss anything.

'Makes me no difference,' Dalton said, 'but why not just keep skipping ahead and have your diploma in two or three years?'

'I don't know,' Sander shrugged. 'No reason, I guess,' and he returned to his mound of new potatoes and sausage.

'Uh-huh. Who is she?'

Her name was Alejandra Sandoval, and she happened to be in the eighth grade when Sander showed up.

Alejandra's grandparents immigrated north from Chiapas,

Mexico, in the years after World War II, so her family didn't have as much of a history in Dixon, or with the Grants, as did most of the people in town. Obviously they were accustomed to seeing the big people around, but they hadn't yet achieved that inborn acceptance of living among giants. It's one thing to go about your business at the feet of these men, keeping yourself from staring more times than not. It's another thing altogether to imagine yourself in a relationship with one. And a bigger leap again to being at peace with your little girl dating one. When Dalton went through this with Frank, at least he didn't have the cultural barrier to contend with. He did not envy his son.

Jaime Sandoval wanted his daughter to find a nice Hispanic boy. His wife, Clarita, couldn't agree more. Dixon had a thriving Hispanic community and there were plenty of respectable families to choose from. What's more, they were all, so far as Clarita knew, Catholic. Most of them went to their church, the same one Sander visited some months ago. Alejandra didn't see him sitting back there, but Jaime and Clarita did. Now, rumor had it, Sander was going to that church full of weirdos over on Eden Drive. Which wasn't entirely accurate. He had been there once. Though, had anyone asked him, he would not have denied that he intended to return.

As for Allie, she was smart, gorgeous, strong-willed and not afraid of much. Sander couldn't think of a thing to add to that recipe. He approached her on the fourth day of school. By the fourth week, he'd already decided to quit skipping grades and he told her as much. Inside of two months, they were an item. At school, that is. They weren't up to letting the townsfolk see them together. This was chiefly because Jaime had already heard the talk and he absolutely forbade his daughter to go on a date with the boy.

Through Clarita, he issued several edicts regarding Sander, but it's not like either of them could go to class with Allie. What Jaime could do, though, was keep her working at the family store every waking hour that she didn't spend in school. Clarita could keep her off the telephone and sort of accidentally search every cubic inch of the girl's room while changing her bed linens. This was their strategy and Allie was not blind to it.

Sander had a strategy in mind as well, but his relied heavily on timing. Half the school year had passed before he was able to implement his design. Dalton had appropriated funds from the budget and they were replacing that fence in the northeast corner, the one Bart was worried about, when Sander brought up the subject.

'Dad, would you and mamma like to meet Allie sometime?'

'Is it serious between you two?'

They progressed at a walking pace, leapfrogging one past the other, picking up the T-posts where they had spaced them out, holding them plumb with one hand, then crashing down a single blow with the post driver in the other hand. Like so many of their daily tasks, no machine made could do it faster than him and his boy, and that alone was proof to Dalton that these very things were what Grants should do. Their conversation continued in spurts as they passed behind each other.

'I don't want any other.'

Sander said that just as Dalton was on a downstroke and he heard the slightly off sound of the whack. Dalton mumbled something, jerked the crooked post from the ground and straightened it.

'What about her? What does she want?'

'Marriage. Children. Nice little house south of the border where we can raise goats. They eat a lot of goat down there.'

Dalton was standing still. 'Quit joking around. You've been steady for a while now. Your mom and I aren't deaf. I don't think these are unreasonable questions.'

'Seriously? Okay. Guess what Jaime does.'

Dalton already knew what the Sandovals did. 'They own that little hardware store outside of town. Don't they?'

They were regaining their momentum now.

'Yep. And Allie says they can order any feed on the market. I've found the one we need to try. It aint the most expensive. It aint the cheapest. But it's the one for us. We can order it by the pallet and have it in a week. They don't have to stock it, so we get a break on the price.'

Cattle feed had been the subject of much debate between them for going on a year now. Hay sales had played a key role in digging them out of the financial crunch resultant of the semen storage operation. However, it had taken its toll in return. Obviously they couldn't allow their stock to feed in the fields dedicated to hay production. They could rotate back into those fields after a crop was harvested, but the nutrient value available from a fallow field, having been conditioned for rapid growth and recently harvested, fell short of what Grant cattle needed. This was especially true for their growers and calves during the critical June to October period when the quality of the forage naturally drops anyway.

Dalton was no stranger to feeding grain. Will had gotten a little ambitious once, way back, and kept a few dozen more breeders than the land could easily support. It was a calculated gamble, but the weather didn't cooperate. Rather than put the animals down, Dalton's father made a deal with Pete Lawson's father; beef for grain. The grain was so expensive that Will's gamble was a wash, that's what Dalton remembered.

Sander kept telling him that the new stuff was both cheaper and more nutrient-dense, so you needed less of it. It was the science behind the new stuff that bothered Dalton. He didn't understand when Sander rambled on about organic supplementation and optimizing genetic potential through protein and phosphorous ratio management. Or something like that. How can you make grain better? No getting around it, though. Something had to be done.

'You priced feed?' he asked Sander.

'Yeah.'

'You didn't think I needed to be in on that?'

'That's what this is, dad. Me filling you in.'

'We've always taken our business to McCoy's or Lawson Farm and Ranch. We don't know anything about the Sandoval store.'

'It's a True Value franchise. And we know these T-posts came from there.'

'Do what? Who said you could go off and do that?'

'I saved us twenty cents apiece. You want me to take em back?'

So that's how it would go down, thought Dalton, just like in the old days. Balanced symbiotic relationship is the euphemism – between people on the one hand, between pocketbooks on the other. He wasn't especially happy with that because he saw it as a step backward. When he was a boy, his daddy told him stories of their ancestors vying for acceptance among the locals by taking all their business to the old town merchants. It's the easiest way to get on their good side, he said. Show them you trust them, you can help them. Dalton thought even then that it seemed a crass and insubstantial bond, and that's without romantic entanglements complicating things. The numbers made sense, though, and

Dalton soon relented. As far as Sander's thing with Jaime's daughter, well, he wished the boy luck.

It wasn't long before Pete Lawson spotted Sander pulling a trailer of feed and supplies from the True Value parking lot. Or he heard about it. Or he suspected it and started asking around. An operation like Grant Beef can't hide much in a town the size of Dixon. Sander saw his dad on the phone one day at lunch, shaking his head, catching a ration of hell from somebody while his steak grew cold on the plate. When he figured out it was Pete, he stood and asked for the phone. Dalton had always hated the telephone and was none too sore about getting Pete out of his ear and sitting back down to his plate.

'Mr Lawson? This is Sander.'

'I know you, son. I was just explaining to your father that you don't cut a relationship like ours for the sake of a girlfriend. I had no opportunity to bid when you started buying feed. No offense, but that aint right. She's a good girl. They're good people, I'm sure, but–'

'You got your books in front of you, Mr Lawson?' Then, 'Go get em. I'll wait.'

Sander stood there eating a sirloin with his free hand and when Pete was back on the phone, he told him the brand name of the feed, precisely how much they ordered and at what intervals, off the top of his head. He waited again and exchanged a glance with his dad.

'No sir,' said Sander. 'I need your best price. I got lunch waiting.'

Pete gave him a good deal, cut his margin to near zero and told Sander so.

'Mr Lawson–' He was interrupted, then continued, 'Okay,

Pete, you were straight with me and I'm gonna do you the same. That's better than fifteen percent higher than what we're paying now. We can't afford it.'

'That stuff, the protein supplement, comes from overseas. No way I can compete with a national chain like True Value and you know it, Sander. I can't work for nothing.'

'No sir. Nobody's asking you to.' He sucked steak juice off his fingers. 'But Grant Beef aint a hobby. We have a bottom line too.' Pause. 'I can understand why you think that, and I'll tell Alejandra you think she's a nice little Mexican girl. But one thing's got nothing to do with the other. We clear on that?'

Dalton watched and ate, noticing how comfortable his son was in this role, how unperturbed by Lawson's rants and pleas and inappropriate remarks. When Sander sat back down to his plate, he asked him, 'How'd he leave it?'

Sander shrugged. 'Hung up on me.'

Jo was walking in from the den. 'Who hung up on you?'

'Pete Lawson,' Dalton told her.

'What on earth for?'

'It's ranch business, honey.'

She brought them more bread and tea, then started cleaning the kitchen.

Dalton asked, 'How are you getting on with Jaime?'

'He's a very good businessman, a straight talker. He trusts me on his forklift, which is good, and none of our orders have been late.'

'And?'

'And we don't talk about that. Not yet, anyway.'

Friday rolled around again and Jason showed up that evening with a check made out to Sander Grant in the amount of five hundred dollars.

'What's this for?' asked Sander.

'One of your paintings,' Jason told him with a smile.

'Which one?'

'You choose. He doesn't care.'

'Who is this person?'

'A buyer in New York. Scott Jacob Paulson. I've shown in his gallery.'

'Why would he buy art he hasn't seen?'

'They do it all the time. He's loaded and I told him some about you.'

'Like what? What did you tell him?' Sander asked.

'That you were better than me.'

Sander turned the check over in his hand. 'So I just pick out whichever one I want to get rid of and send it?'

'You can do it that way if five hundred dollars is all you want. Or, you can let me help you pick out your most outstanding piece of work and sell it to him for less than it's worth. When he asks for more – which he will – the price is no longer five hundred dollars. And he won't expect it to be.'

All Sander could think of was what he could buy Allie with a couple hundred dollars and how he could hide a reconditioned arc welder in the shop beside the barn. Dalton wouldn't be happy about it, but their welder had given up the ghost last week and things needed fixing. Maybe he could knock around the replacement and scuff it with a wire brush so it looked like the old one once it rusted a bit. His dad never looked very closely at the tools.

He and Jason spent their hour together debating which of Sander's inventory represented his most mature, balanced work.

There were dozens, years worth, stacked and leaning against the walls. They settled on *Deception*, an enormous oil on canvas depicting a man in work clothes, head down in a pasture but facing the viewer. In the background stood a black bull. At first glance, it appeared the bull was some distance behind the man; its relative size forced a depth perspective judgment upon the viewer. Jason said it was nearly flawless in composition and bleeding emotion. That's what would sell it. However, when somebody – the gallery, the buyer, or some subsequent owner – realized the man's fingertips were touching the bull's shoulder, the viewers' perceptions would crumble and they would suddenly realize they were staring at a giant. Jason predicted it would resale for several times the initial price, and he said Sander simply had to accept the loss. For now.

They wrapped the canvas carefully and Jason said he would ship it tomorrow, COD. 'They can't expect us to pay for shit like that,' he said. 'And I would be expecting to hear from Scott Jacob shortly, if I were you.'

Dixon True Value closed at five o'clock on Saturday. Allie always rode to work with Jaime and, after cleaning up, closing out the register, and doing whatever stocking remained from Thursday's delivery truck, they were generally home by seven or eight. That's a bit late to pay a call on someone, Sander realized, but Sunday was out of the question and he could not wait until Monday.

Sander stood on their doorstep at ten past eight, holding a bouquet of flowers. He took a deep breath and rang the bell. The porch light came on but the door didn't open. Gnats buzzed in his face. He could feel an eye staring at him through the peephole and heard footsteps receding into the house, then more footsteps approaching the door. Allie opened it.

'Sander? I wish you had called.'

'Your parents would've told me not to come.'

She looked at the flowers and whispered, 'Bring them to me at school.'

'I can't. I mean, no, that's not–'

'We're having dinner.'

'I'm sorry.'

Clarita walked into the foyer behind Allie. 'That's long enough to tell him we're eating.'

Allie looked down and shook her head.

Her mother said, 'Take the flowers, Alejandra, and close the door.' She did not acknowledge Sander.

'They aren't for her, Mrs Sandoval. They're for you.' He held them up, but didn't dare reach over Allie and across the threshold. 'Should I leave them on the porch?'

She stepped forward and stood beside her daughter. The smile on her face reminded Sander of something Jason told him a long time ago. There's no feeling in a curved line, he'd said, it's just a line.

Clarita took the bouquet. 'Thank you, Sander. They are splendid.' She excused herself with a nod and, as she walked away, '*Dos minutos*, Alejandra.'

Allie waited, then whispered, 'You can't bribe her with flowers.'

'Not trying to.' Sander pulled a purple felt box from his pocket and hurriedly said, 'Just buying time. This is for you. Go eat your dinner.'

Allie stared at the gold bracelet.

'I can't believe it.' She looked up at him. 'Thank you so much. I'm very sorry about–' She glanced over her shoulder.

'Don't be. I love you. See you Monday.'

Allie watched him drive away.

Sander had already bought the welder earlier that day, but he couldn't bring himself to bust it up. It was too fine a machine. The subterfuge wouldn't have worked anyway, as this was a bigger model. He kept it in the truck that night and, before sunrise Sunday morning, he hauled out the broken welder and plopped the new one in its place. His dad could gripe if he wanted, but things needed fixing and Sander resolved he could spend his own money however he saw fit.

The plan was to drop the old welder off at the dump on his way to First Unitarian that morning. He was hungry for another of Roger's lectures, and possibly a few answers about that newspaper article. He still didn't understand what he was supposed to get from that. He could be home by noon or a little after and help his dad brand some calves. Dalton had other plans. He was sitting at the dining table when Sander came down the stairs in his nice clothes.

From the kitchen, Jo said, 'Breakfast is ready. Orange juice, baby?'

'No, mamma, thanks.'

'You ... going to church this morning?' asked Dalton.

'Yeah, I thought I'd go over and–' He noticed the ranch ledger book on the table in front of his father. It was massive and leather bound. There were several of these books, worn and yellowed, somewhere in his parents' bedroom, but Sander recognized this as the current one. 'What's up?'

'Are they expecting you? What I mean to say is, could you skip service today? I'd like to talk to you about something.'

'Sure. No, they aint waiting around for me. Something wrong?'

'After breakfast,' said Dalton. 'I'm hungry.'

Jo began ferrying food to the table. She placed a gallon of milk and a quart Mason jar in front of each of them, then brought her own plate.

'I ran out of eggs,' she said. She had fried them and it looked like there were only two dozen on the platter. 'So make em last. I'll go to the store later.'

'It's plenty,' Sander told her, and filled his plate with ham steaks, grits, and waffles while Dalton started on the eggs.

Jo cleared the table when they were done and stacked the dishes in the sink.

'I'll do those later,' she said. 'I'm going to have a shower.'

She knew, Sander thought. Whatever it was his dad wanted to discuss, she knew it was serious. Dalton wiped his mouth and opened the ledger. He studied it a moment before he began.

'We've been on your feeding plan now for several months, son. Starting, like you said, with our finishing stock, heifers and steers. You'll recall that was your doing, and I trusted you on it.'

'It's too soon to see any tangible results.'

'No it aint. It's already there, black and white.' He paused to consider, then, 'You know we sold fifty head last week. You helped load em.'

'The ones we sold didn't even go through a whole finishing cycle. Come on, dad. Gimme a break.'

'Full cycle or not, Sander, it's not panning out like you thought it would.'

He slid the open book across the table to his son. As always, the pink stockyard receipt was clipped to the top of the page and it itemized weight delivered, percentage lean, and USDA grading. These numbers then carried over to price per pound. Sander could not believe what he was seeing. He flipped back to the previous pink slip. The numbers varied slightly by lot sample, but his rough estimate of the latest sale gave an average of fifty pounds more beef yield per animal and an increase of four percent lean meat.

'I had no idea,' Sander said. 'I mean, I knew it would work, but not like this. Not this quick.'

'Well, as long as you can admit when you're wrong. I hope you got that trait from me, but I doubt it.' Sander started to say something. Dalton held up his hand. 'Listen, son. I took control of the place when my father died. He had run it from the day he buried granddad. It's how we've always done it. The business is different now, though. Techniques and things are changing faster than I can keep up. Opportunities don't linger around until a person decides to grab on. When you miss them, they're gone.'

'All this,' Sander pointed to the book, 'feeding patterns, cycles, ratios – it's all at the library. I didn't come up with it.'

'But you went and found it. You badgered me until I listened, and you made it work. That's because you're different, too. Bigger, stronger, and a heck of a lot smarter than any of us. So it's time to part with custom. You've already decided to quit school after next year anyway. When you do, I want you to take over as ranch foreman.'

'Dad–'

'I aint going anywhere. I reckon I've got a few things left to teach you, and I'll be right there beside you when you start making our decisions. I won't see us get passed up by some other operation because my thick-headed ways are holding us back.'

'Alright. I think you're jumping the gun, but okay.'

'Explain things to me, talk to me and let me know what you're doing. I'll do the best I can to understand the why of it all. When I can't, you just tell me the how part. Will you do that?'

'Yes, sir.'

'Can you do it without forgetting I'm your father?'

'Yes, sir.'

'Good.' Dalton looked at his watch. 'Is there time for you to get to church?'

'Not really, but it's okay. They'll be there again next Sunday.'

'You wanna burn some calves then?'

'Yeah. Let me change clothes.'

It was a week before Scott Jacob called from The Paulson Gallery.

'Good afternoon,' he said, 'Could I speak to Sander Grant, please?'

'Who's calling?' Jo asked.

'Scott Jacob Paulson. I'm an art dealer in New York. I recently purchased one of Mr Grant's works.'

'Yes, Scott. I remember. I'll try to find him.'

'Scott Jacob,' the man corrected, but Jo had already put the phone on the counter.

Five minutes later, Sander came in from the barn wiping grease from his hands.

'This is Sander.'

'Mr Grant – Scott Jacob Paulson here, from *The* Paulson Gallery.' He placed a slight, well-practiced emphasis on 'the.' 'How are you?'

'Busy. No complaints about that.'

'Indeed! It never ends for the gifted few. I love it! Something exciting underway?'

Sander suppressed a laugh. This guy was too animated, so incredibly absorbed in his own little cosmos.

'Oh yeah,' he told the art dealer. 'Tractor's bouncing a little with the new manure spreader. That's the big thing that slings cow shit to fertilize the alfalfa. I think it's got too much draft on the lower link of the three-point. Fairly exciting, I guess.'

Silence on the line.

'I'm sorry,' said Paulson. 'Is this Sander Grant, the artist?'

'No, sir. This is Sander Grant, the rancher. But I think you have one of my paintings.'

'Not anymore, Mr Grant. It sold before I could hang it. Jason was right about you. I won't keep you from your manure, just calling to see if perhaps you would like to give us a look at your portfolio.'

'I don't have a portfolio,' said Sander. 'I think I have a Polaroid around here somewhere. Is it pictures you're after?'

'Um, yes, I suppose. Or, better yet, might there be a convenient time we could come view your work? In your studio? I'm concerned that Polaroids wouldn't do justice to the pieces.'

'If you wanna come all the way down here to see my stuff, I'll make some time. Just call when you're on the way.'

'Terribly forward of me. And, thank you.'

'No big deal,' said Sander. 'Jason knows where I live. See you soon.'

It was two more weeks after they left the ranch, Scott Jacob Paulson and the older bespectacled man slinking on his heels, when the press started calling. Paulson had loaded six of Sander's canvases in his rental van after they agreed on price.

'Start high,' Jason had told Sander. 'The man's flying all the way from New York just to have a peek.'

He evidently didn't start high enough, because Scott Jacob

began writing the check as soon as 'fifteen hundred dollars' came out of Sander's mouth.

'A *piece*,' clarified Sander, which brought a chuckle from Scott Jacob and the slinker.

Looking at the nine-thousand-dollar check, Sander had to wonder what price these men would put on his work. The first reporter, from *The Dallas Morning News*, answered that question for him.

'The Paulson has two left, as of yesterday,' said the reporter. 'They're not marked. Presumably they'll go to the best offer. The last one brought twenty thousand. Did you know that?'

'No.'

'How does it make you feel?'

Stupid is what came to mind. Instead, Sander replied, 'Good. Makes me feel good.'

'Any chance for an interview? In person? Maybe a photograph for the article?'

There it was. The real question: Twenty grand for the painting, or twenty grand for anything painted by a giant? Didn't really matter, Sander only got fifteen hundred dollars. That was validation enough for the images on the canvas.

'I don't think so,' he told the reporter. 'Nobody in Dallas cares what I look like.'

'Pardon me, Sander, but they do. And not just in Dallas. It's no trouble. I won't take ten minutes of your time. I'm right here in Dixon, Motel 6.'

Sander heard a knock on the door. Jo was shopping in town and Dalton was on the back feed lot.

'I've gotta go. Thanks for the interest.'

He looked out the peephole and saw a man holding a tablet,

a camera slung over his shoulder. Sander eased out the patio door and disappeared across the field. The articles came out anyway, some of them syndicated and all of them with a mysterious slant regarding the artist. Somebody had dug up some old school pictures, a few shots of him in grade school yearbooks, and it appeared one enterprising photographer with an inordinately heavy lens had managed to capture him lifting a calf over a fence. The shot had been taken from the street.

Jo took to screening his calls like a trained sentry and they developed the habit of unplugging the telephone before dinner, leaving the cord dangling until after breakfast the following morning. There weren't many people brazen enough to be bothersome on their doorstep, but the postman occasionally had to bring up those letters that wouldn't cram into the mailbox. Sander read few of them, and lost interest in the reviews with their repetition of phrases such as 'neoteric naturalism' and 'astonishing magic realism'. These folks had very limited vocabularies and liked to quote one another.

For the most part, all this buzz thrilled Jo, the annoyance notwithstanding, and Dalton tolerated it remarkably well so long as people stayed out of his pastures. Sander liked the money. He liked the fact that people liked his work, but he could do without the attention. Applying the lesson from his dad's price control methods with Grant Beef, Sander rationed those remaining pieces, selling exclusively through The Paulson once he renegotiated his price, and otherwise had little to do with painting for a while. Eventually, there trickled in only a call or two and maybe a few letters when a new piece hit the market or an older one resold at auction.

By midpoint of his ninth grade year, Sander had come to some decisions. He had ninety-seven thousand dollars in the bank and a new truck rigged much the same as his dad's, except his was built at the factory that way. He had, despite opposition from Dalton, replenished the coffers of Grant Beef to a comfortable level and they steadily built upon that. A herd of over five hundred head was within reach for the first time in two generations. All while the name Sander Grant remained on the lips of artists and aficionados across the country and beyond. High school seemed like a fool's errand now, to him and his teachers.

Moreover, though Allie's father was not impressed by Sander's notoriety and success as an artist, Jaime had come to respect him as a man of business, a man of integrity, and a man who might support his daughter. The cultural divide was as wide as ever. Yet, in light of Allie's determination to stick by Sander, Jaime eventually acquiesced to a proper courtship, a public one. Now that he had Jaime's permission to see her socially, he first told his parents, then told Allie that he wouldn't be coming back to Dixon High after the Christmas break. Nobody could argue.

The other decision was not so manifest. At least, not to Dalton.

His father didn't care whether Sander finished the ninth grade or the tenth before he took over as ranch foreman. Education wasn't an issue, he was ready. It was his first proposed act as foreman that Dalton had a few concerns about.

'Since I can remember,' Sander told his dad, 'we've been busting our rumps around here trying not to fail. As opposed,' he added, 'to getting ahead.'

Dalton looked to see that his boy had the new wheel on the lugs and all the lug nuts finger-tight, then set the front of the truck down. Sander felt around behind him for the tire tool.

'There have been good times,' Dalton said.

Sander tightened the nuts while his dad threw the flat tire in the bed.

'Don't get defensive. Nothing you could've done about the weather, and there weren't as many options back then.'

He rose from his knees and he kept on rising. He was at least as tall as Dalton now, maybe an inch taller. It was Sander studying his father now with new eyes. Could've been an effect of the setting sun, or just some dust, but he thought he noticed a few gray hairs. He wondered if the slight shadows beneath his dad's cheekbones were always present these days, or just when he was worn out. Come to think of it, how many times had he seen the big man worn out?

Sander brushed the dirt off his pants. With a sweep of the tire tool, he indicated everything outside their fences.

'They bank on Grant Beef. How many restaurants you reckon we support? How many meat markets set their prices based on our production?' Dalton took the iron from him and dropped it in the tool box. 'I'm saying that our stock is a commodity unto itself and I want to capitalize on that.'

'Where I didn't.'

'Yes you did. You saved the place. And I'm gonna take what you saved and run with it. Isn't that why you gave me the job?'

'I don't remember anything about running. Where is it you wanna go?'

'Global,' said Sander. 'Lookit, do you know what Kobe beef is?'

'Like Colby cheese?'

'K-o-b-e. It's from Japan, the black Tajima-ushi breed of Wagyu cattle.'

'Ten bucks says you can't spell the rest of them words.'

'I'm not kidding, dad. We've known for a long time that USDA prime grading doesn't do us a bit of good. Otto Ritchey over there can get his polled Brangus graded prime if he butchers them early enough.'

Dalton bristled at the mention of the Ritchey operation. 'Maybe. He can't call it Grant Beef, though.'

'No, and neither can anybody else. But do you think there's anybody over in Japan talking about US Department of Agriculture labels right now?'

'Son, I don't even know why we're doing it.'

'I'll show you why.' Sander looked at his wristwatch in the fading light and said, 'Mamma's in there right now cooking dinner. I got us each a Kobe steak.'

'Just one?'

'Wait a minute. Mamma's gonna put those on our plates right alongside beef we raised. I'll kiss your ass if you can tell the difference.'

Jo called to them from the patio.

'Don't talk like that around your mother,' Dalton said.

Jo took her seat while they washed up. The table was already set and piled high. She was privy to Sander's game and eager to watch the show. Dalton sat down and prodded the eight steaks before him, thinking about all those foreign words and what a Japanese cow might look like. The cooked meat looked the same, top to bottom. Sander took his seat. They passed the potatoes au gratin and the biscuit platter, then, without another word, began to eat.

Even for a Grant man, Sander ate fast. He went through food like a herd of goats in a dooryard, so he and Jo finished at about the same time. She had two cobblers staying warm in the oven and they could all smell them, but neither she nor Sander budged until Dalton looked up. There was a single bite of meat left in the center of his plate. He pointed to it with his fork.

'That's not Grant Beef,' he said. 'But other than ours, it's the best I've ever had.' He tried out the word for himself, 'Kobe,' then took his last bite.

Sander grinned while Jo got up to fetch dessert.

'I'm glad you liked it, dad. Cost me eighty bucks.'

'Oh, there's more?'

'No, sir. Your steak cost eighty dollars. So did mine.'

'Say that again?'

'You heard me. And it's not spoiling on the racks. You have to wait your turn when you order it.' Sander took the last biscuit as Jo picked up the platter. 'Global,' he said, and popped the biscuit in his mouth.

Sander's plan was twofold, though it wasn't complicated. As Dalton should've expected, his boy's research was comprehensive. After the cobbler was gone, Sander presented him with a list of meat distributors he'd already contacted, each company had a longstanding and significant presence overseas. Sander's notes took into account the cost of outsourced distribution as well as a noticeable hit on tonnage, as they would have to sell younger stock. This was the near-term portion of his plan and the bottom line didn't suffer much for it. Projecting the numbers out a mere five years showed a three hundred percent profit increase.

In tandem, Sander insisted they must stay ahead of the curve in the domestic market. This meant dry aging, targeted at the upscale restaurants on the East and West Coasts, and to some extent circumventing the meat packers. Dalton knew about dry aging. Nearly every cattleman did. In the winter, they often hung butchered halves in the barn as a treat. Let it cure, cut it down, and enjoy it over the holidays. But scarce few operations ever sold dry-aged beef because the cost of year-round refrigeration, the manpower required, and the loss of total weight was simply too much to absorb. The way Sander explained it, this would be their longer-term investment, and he was prepared and willing to manage both aspects simultaneously.

'I figure,' he told Dalton, 'another ten hired hands would do it.'

'Can I make a suggestion?'

'Sure.'

'Start out hiring three. Try to find Larry and Danny Smitherman, if they're still around. I had to let them go last year, but they're real good workers. Add more if it gets where we can't handle it.'

7

Larry Smitherman was looking for work at the time and said he could start the Monday after Sander's call. His brother Danny would soon be done with his job on an oil rig west of Henderson and sent word he'd be back on the ranch come Friday. Both brothers were elated to get the call. Sander's third new hire, a thirty-year-old man named Michael Spears, had never worked for the Grants before. He hailed from Fort Worth and his notice pinned to the hardware store bulletin board claimed eleven years experience with cattle. They agreed on wages over the phone and Sander told him to show up Friday.

'What time?' asked Spears.

'When it's daylight, you need to already be here.'

So, with Javier, their longest-standing employee, his son Anthony, the Smitherman brothers and Spears, Sander had his starting workforce of five. He and Dalton made seven. It would do for now.

Monday morning, Sander told Javier, 'Take the surveyor's transit and lay us out a feed lot, four square, adjacent to the other one.'

'Just four acres?' Javier asked.

'For now. It's all the fence we've got. Then get everybody driving T-posts down there. Space em out and make em last. Dad and I will put dead men on the corners to hold the tension.'

Dalton already had some boulders in mind for that, ones he'd been meaning to get out of the creek for years.

'Yes, sir,' said Javier to Sander.

As he and his son walked through the gate, Anthony said, 'Is he the boss now?'

'You saw Mr Dalton standing right there,' said Javier. 'If he wanted to tell us otherwise, he would've.'

Meanwhile, Sander and Dalton would spend the day cutting their best stock from the south pasture. The man from Argos Meat Distributors wanted a look at what he would be representing. He was flying in from British Columbia in a few months, giving Sander the time he felt he needed to have everything in place. They had several dozen handsome calves on hand, more mature beef that could stand a little conditioning, and Sander wanted all of them in a feed lot as much as possible until the Argos man arrived. First impressions being as they are, he also wanted the meat cooler humming, whether there was beef hanging in it or not.

By Wednesday, the new lot was fenced and Javier had staked off a pad beside the barn where Sander had determined to put the meat cooler. They could not afford even a used commercial unit big enough to hang the weight of beef Sander had in mind. He had books, though, on insulation methods, air locks, and refrigeration. Much of what he needed to know he had learned from the semen facility. Dalton trusted him, but when he saw the size of the pad Javier and Anthony had laid out, it scared him. Sander saw it.

'Easy, dad. Stages. We'll get the concrete down first and let it sit there until we can afford to frame it.' Dalton nodded. Good plan. 'Then, when it's starting to come along, we can start on our slaughter facility.' And Dalton's trepidation returned in a breaking wave.

'Come on,' Sander told him, 'we've got digging to do.'

Michael Spears turned out to be an industrious hand, if a little cocky. It was fortunate for him that he worked hard because, among this crew, a good-enough effort would stand out like a leghorn rooster in a dog race. Still, Javier didn't cotton to the fella and, as Dalton was knocking off for lunch that first day, he pulled the big man aside and shared his thoughts.

'That one,' said Javier.

'Spears?'

'He's aint right, boss. I don't know what it is, but–' He began again. 'My wife's brother, Miguel, he's a good worker. Knows cattle. I trust him. This Spears, he bugs me.'

'Seems to me like he's pulling his load. You need to talk to Sander about this.'

Javier had a good relationship with Dalton and considered they were friends. He had worked this ranch since before his own son was born and long before Jo got pregnant, so he knew them all very well. Yet, he was hesitant to second-guess Sander on his first week as foreman. He said nothing more about it.

The big trucks started rolling in early the next day to pour the concrete. Sander was happy to defer to Javier's knowledge of flatwork and under the Mexican man's direction they had footings in and the slab floated before dusk. Spears hadn't screwed up anything, but it was only his second day. Javier was watching him.

Sander could not keep his dad from working on Sunday, though he insisted the hired help take the day off. He intended to push them, to wring every wage dollar out of these guys before he had to hire more, and he did not want them burning out. Besides, Sander had put off going back to First Unitarian long enough. It was on his mind more and more lately.

Sander purposely left early Sunday morning because he wanted to talk to Roger before his lecture, if possible. Roger was standing on the steps of the church smoking a cigarette when he drove up. There were no other cars there.

'I thought you quit,' Sander said.

'I said I tried. It didn't take. I'll have one now and again.' He studied it as though it was his first. 'Stress drives me to vice.' He tipped the ash and put it to his lips, drawing hard enough on the butt that the end glowed even in the sunlight.

Sander noticed he did look a little frazzled today. Then again, he didn't know the man. *Maybe this is how he always looks when he's not in front of the congregation.* Whatever, it seemed none of Sander's business.

'Nephilim?' he said to Roger.

'Yeah.' Roger thumped his cigarette into the gravel but made no move to go inside. He kept looking at the butt down there, like he was thinking there might have been more in it. 'Your mother talks to God?'

'Is that what Jason told you?' Then, 'Jason says you talk to God, too.'

'Sometimes. Has Josephine talked to Him lately?'

'I'm ... not sure where you're going with this, Roger. I guess most Christians talk to the Lord.'

'Don't be coy, Sander, please.' That set Sander on edge. Roger saw it. 'I know we're talking about the same thing. She hears the voice of God.'

'She says she does. I haven't heard it.'

'And you doubt her?'

'Roger, I don't think this is any of your business and it's starting to piss me off. What is it you're after?'

'You mentioned Nephilim to her, in passing, or she saw it or something. Am I right?'

'I asked her and dad both if they knew anybody by that name.'

'You need to ask her again. Not about the name. Just ask her if God's had anything to say lately. Would you do that?'

'Absolutely not. If she had something to tell me, she would.'

'Maybe not,' said Roger.

Two cars pulled onto the gravel at the same time. A pickup truck was close behind.

'I have to prepare,' Roger said, and turned to go inside.

Sander stood there wondering whether he'd just been uninvited to attend service. Joyce, Neil, and Carla Rae climbed the steps together.

'You gonna stand out here all morning?'

Sander didn't know which one said it. More tires crunched in the gravel behind him. He went in and took his seat. Jason sauntered in a few minutes later and sat down beside him as the pews gradually filled.

'Good to have you back.'

Sander turned to him. 'How long have you known Roger?'

'He moved here two or three years ago, donated this house to start the church. The bottom half, anyway. You forget your Bible?'

'Don't need it,' said Sander. Then, 'Seems like you told me you went to another church. Back when we first started talking about it.'

'Yeah, you're right,' Jason recalled. 'I was driving to Longview at the time. Calvary Chapel.'

Sander lowered his voice as the congregation settled in. 'Then you found this place, or Roger found you?'

'I think he came by the studio. Why?'

'And how much have you told him about me and my family? Private things.' Sander was looking straight ahead.

A shocked and wounded aura radiated from Jason as he stared at the side of Sander's face. Sander felt sure any response would strike him as pitifully sanctimonious, so he was glad Roger was coming down the stairs.

Today's service began rather lackluster in presentation, at least compared to the only other one Sander had seen. Roger invited less participation this time and he moved through the text more quickly. Sander had no problem keeping up, but he could tell that a few points needed to be revisited, broken down so the whole congregation might follow by the light of their own logic, from question to revelation. This is what had impressed Sander so much at his last visit.

Instead, Roger hit the key points squarely on the head, then moved on, like it was a review. And maybe it was – this story of Abraham's willingness to murder Isaac because God told him to – Sander couldn't know. Yes, Roger again held his audience enrapt and displayed a knowledge of scripture that would shame a savant. But there was something building in his tone that ... What was it?

'"Take now thy son, thine *only* son Isaac, whom thou *lovest*,"' quoted Roger, punctuating the air with his chalk. 'Just so we know, so there can be no illusions that Abraham had any grudge against the kid; God said take him up there on the mountain and kill him. Not because he had transgressed against the Lord. Not for any reason save testing Abraham. And without comment, Abraham saddled his ass the next morning and set off. He lied to his boy on the way up. Isaac wondered, "... but where is the lamb for a burnt offering?" I can just hear him: "Daddy, we forgot the lamb."

'His father told him not to worry about it because, "God will provide himself a lamb." Now, do you think once Isaac figured out *he* was the lamb, he just shrugged and climbed up on that altar? I mean, would you? Nuh-uh. Says in the next verse that Abraham bound him. Tied him up. Subdued and forced him down, in other words.'

Roger stopped and looked down as though Isaac's wriggling body were on an imaginary altar before him. He stilled the boy with his empty hand and raised his chalk into the air like a knife, then stood like that while he met eyes with the congregation.

Sander knew what he was sensing before. There was anger here. Bile behind the words, barely disguised as a bit of drama for educational effect. Roger gave a half-hearted smile, lowered his chalk and the scene vanished. So, seemingly, did the anger.

'Of course, Abe doesn't butcher his son,' continued Roger, with a decidedly professorial tone. 'We all know God stops him. The conventional lesson gleaned from this story is unquestioning obedience. As such, Abraham's is a fine example, but that message accounts only for the God perspective. Let's take a look at the thing from Isaac's point of view.'

As soon as Roger bid them good afternoon, Sander was on his way home. He hadn't seen his grandparents in so long, he was elated that their car was in the drive when he pulled up. For the time, he forgot all about his brief conversation with Roger on the church steps.

'Good lord, Doris,' said Frank as Sander walked in the door, 'look at this monster!' Sander passed his father in the kitchen and Frank said, 'Damn you people make a guy feel like a mouse turd.'

Doris wiped her hands on a dish towel and reached up to hug her grandson. She whispered, 'He's been into the whiskey this morning. We'll get some food in his belly.' Then, pushing back so she could have a look at him, 'You look nice. Hungry?'

'Yes, ma'am. I'll just go change.'

Frank didn't sober up much during lunch, mainly owing to the Jack Daniel's he kept adding to his iced tea. No matter, it was good to see and be seen by all. What with all that had been going on of late, their regular Sunday meal together had unintentionally fallen by the wayside. As Doris rounded up her husband and her Tupperware of leftovers, they resolved as a family to remedy that. Lunch on Sundays, at the ranch, unless there was some good excuse.

Once they were gone, Sander said, 'Grandma doesn't look so good.'

'Yeah,' said Jo, 'she hasn't been getting out much and she's complaining about her legs hurting. When she called last night, I thought it would be nice to have them over. Forgot to tell you this morning.'

'No, it's great.' Sander pondered on a diplomatic way to say this, couldn't find one and so, 'She's gained a lot of weight.'

'I know. It's got me worried there's something she's not telling me.'

'Diabetes,' said Sander.

'She won't go to a doctor. I think it may be why dad's drinking so much.'

Dalton said, 'I'm gonna check the troughs.' Before he slid the patio door closed, he added, 'I don't know why you don't just talk to your folks. Easier than trying to guess what somebody's thinking.'

Sander chewed on a toothpick while he collected his thoughts. Jo loaded the dishwasher.

'I need to ask you something, mamma. It's about the church.' That wasn't right. 'No it aint. It's about God.'

Jo stopped. 'Okay.'

'Has He said anything to you lately?'

'Like what?'

'Like anything. Has *He* spoken to you?'

'Yes, He has, Sander. Just the other night.'

'What did He say?'

'I'm not sure it's relevant. Anyway, I had a few things to say myself.' She wiped the same spot on the counter over and over, round and round. 'Sometimes we disagree. I don't just take whatever, you know, He says at face value and I have my concerns and sometimes it takes a good while–'

'Mom?'

'He listens, too, damnit. He listens to me when I make sense.' Sander waited. 'He said that Jason's church is not a good place for you. But only you can decide that, son.'

'He didn't say it in those words, though, did He?'

'I can't remember, exactly.'

His mother was lying and Sander knew it. He also knew it wouldn't do any good to press her for more. Pans and dishes make a different clang when a woman has set her jaw. She had told him enough that he was sure there was more. Roger's cryptic nervousness might not have been as baseless as it seemed. But the conversation was over.

Sander helped his dad prepare for tomorrow morning, ate

dinner standing at the sink, then retired to his bedroom and gazed at the sheetrock ceiling for seven hours.

At breakfast, he and Dalton prepared a list of things they needed to have behind them by week's end and Sander left with the big flat-bed to pick up a load of feed and lumber before the hands arrived.

'Good morning, stranger,' said Allie, as Sander walked into the True Value. 'Haven't seen you in a while.'

'I know. Kinda hectic this past week. I'll get it under control.'

'Come for your feed?'

'Yeah. You working here all day?'

'Dad's sick. The flu or something, so I took off from school. The pallets are out back. Chain's open.'

'Do you feel sick?'

'Nope.'

'Can I have a kiss, then?'

Morning sunlight glinting off a windshield in the parking lot separated them. A man in overalls was making his way to the door.

'Can we go out Friday?' she asked. 'Just a movie or something.'

'Saturday's better. I'll call you.' He turned to leave.

'Hey,' she called, 'you're a good kisser.'

The chain across the loading area in the back was unlocked, like Allie said, but Jaime's forklift wouldn't start. Sander checked the battery connections, the fuel tank, the glow plug leads, and every other part he could get to without stripping off the engine housing. He gave up after the better part of an hour and began loading feed sacks by hand. Each pallet held twenty hundred-pound bags, an even ton, and there were sixteen pallets. It was time consuming work. His next stop was McCoy's to pick up lumber, then he was on his way back. It was nearly noon when he arrived. Michael Spears' pickup was parked in front of the gate, so Sander pulled his loaded rig in behind. He heard voices from the barn and it sounded like the guys were on their break, so he decided to wait until he had something in his belly before telling them, one more time, do not block the gate.

He smelled lunch before he opened the side door to the kitchen. Peering into one of the ovens, he saw it was chicken spaghetti. Lots of cheese, chilies, and diced tomatoes. He went from fairly hungry to ravenous at the sight of the bubbling casserole dishes in there. Then he walked around the corner and saw Dalton sitting at the table, Jo rubbing his neck. Midday sun silhouetted his parents from the patio door behind them, and Sander's immediate thought was that he had never seen his dad this tired. He noticed wrinkles too, about Dalton's brow, down the sides of his face, and deep ones where his throat met his chest. He tried to unsee them.

'You sick? Allie said there's flu going around,' said Sander. 'Jaime never missed a day of–' but by that time, he had reached his end of the table opposite Dalton's and could see by the overhead light a blood stain on his dad's collar. 'What happened?'

His mamma wouldn't look at him. The corner of Dalton's forehead was laid open at the hairline and it looked like he needed stitches.

Dalton said, 'Awe, that jerk blindsided me. Caught me with the edge of a shovel. Shouldn't have turned my back on him.'

'Who did? Where?' Sander turned loose the back of his chair and its heavy oak legs thudded on the tile.

'It's nothing, son. Let's eat.'

'Dad, who hit you?'

'The new guy. Spears. He showed up three hours late and

stinking of booze, so I had to let him go. Javier's already called his brother-in-law to replace him.'

That was Spears' truck Sander had hemmed in at the gate and he knew it. He covered the length of the table and blew by his mom and dad in two strides.

'Don't. He's leaving,' Dalton said, but Sander was already out the door. 'Stop him, Jo.'

She ran out on the patio hollering after her boy.

Michael Spears now sat in the cab of his truck, door open and feet on the ground, drinking from a pint of whiskey. The Smitherman brothers were eating their lunch in the shade of the barn as Spears shouted at them, telling them to go get somebody to move this fuckin' feed wagon so he could go home. When he laughed, he looked like a jackass eating briars. The noise carried across the acres and that laughter was a bellows to the blaze in Sander.

Michael followed Larry's eyes and saw Sander coming, fast. He dropped the bottle on the floorboard, swung his feet into the cab and slammed the door. The truck engine sputtered and died. He was pumping the accelerator like hell, trying the ignition again when Sander reached him. Spears scurried over and slid out the other side when Sander punched through the window, pulled the locked door from its hinges and tossed it. Spears rolled himself over the gate and lit out across the pasture on all fours. He rose, stumbled past the barn, and barreled headlong through the tall grass without looking back.

Sander snapped the steering wheel from the dash of Spears' truck and dropped it. He jerked the bench seat from its bolts and it cartwheeled over his shoulder. He didn't speak or so much as grunt with effort, but he found that whiskey bottle and stuck it in his back pocket. Jo stayed on the patio, well clear of it all and waited for any opportunity to stop it. Sander glanced up to see that Spears had slowed enough to turn and watch, then he bent and flipped the truck over onto its roof. It teetered and stilled itself. Gasoline trickled from the fender. He dusted off his hands and wiped one bloody knuckle on his jeans as he stepped over the gate and walked toward the barn. Spears turned on another burst of speed and disappeared over the nearest hill.

Larry and Danny watched Sander approach, deliberating on whether to take flight themselves. Javier appeared in the bay door and kept Anthony behind him.

Sander asked them, 'Something funny?'

Larry said, 'I told your daddy to break his goddamn neck, Mr Sander. We'd of all said he fell off the hay stacks. Weren't none of us laughing. None.'

Danny stood. 'I'll go catch the sumbitch now if you want.'

Sander met eyes with each of them. 'My father might suffer fools, but I won't. You hear me?'

'Yes sir,' said each of the men. Anthony said it twice, as he was unsure whether Sander heard him.

'And this,' Sander pulled out the whiskey bottle. 'I better not see it again on the job.' He flung it into the trash barrel where it shattered.

Sander turned toward the house and Javier called, 'Mr Sander. Your father told us to leave him alone.'

Back on the patio, Jo said, 'He'll call the sheriff, Sander.'

'Let him. I'll answer for it.' He kept walking.

It seemed like the thing to say to his mother, the thing that would end the discussion, and it did. He knew that Spears wasn't calling any law, because he knew that somebody like that most likely had a criminal record. Somebody who would behave in such a way might even have warrants out for him. And Sander knew that he should've checked on those things before he hired the stranger.

Jo followed her boy into the dining room, but Dalton was no longer there. Sander sat at the table to catch his breath while Jo brought him a clean linen towel for his bloody hand, then set about taking lunch from the ovens.

'When did dad's hair start turning gray, mamma?'

Jo placed the last casserole dish on the range, slammed the oven door and threw her potholders into the sink. She glared at him.

'What!' Sander said.

'Don't you take that tone with me,' she said. 'Do you have any idea how that made your father feel?'

In fact, he did not, so he ignored her question and reiterated his own. 'Are you gonna tell me or not?'

'He's old, Sander. When you get old, everything starts hurting, then you die. Here ends life lesson number one.' She regretted that before it crossed her lips. Anger roiled within her, though, and no apology bubbled to the top. She carried right on lashing him, because he was there. 'If you want people to treat you like some kind of beast, you just keep it up. That stunt out there is a fine start. *Somebody's* going to listen to me, boy. Sooner or later, somebody will listen.'

'What on earth are you talking about, mom?'

She tried to calm herself. She thought it might help to set the table while she talked. 'Nothing. Dalton said he would talk to you about this. He was much older than you when we got married and–' Jo gave it up. Civility was beyond her reach at the moment. She didn't feel like talking to Sander right then. 'Here's an idea – if you have questions about your father, why don't you go ask him? And after you do, turn that truck back over and get it out of my yard. It better not be there tomorrow.'

Dalton was in his bedroom. He'd cleaned himself and changed pants.

'Mamma told me,' Sander said, taking a seat on the bed.

His dad stood in the closet, bare to the waist, looking at clean shirts. The lateral muscles of his back spread like rippled wings from the tight waist of his jeans. Sander watched him shuffle through hanging clothes and saw the chords and engines in his big arms loll around under the skin like lazy animals beneath a blanket. His skin was thinner now, and darker in places. Even the hair on his chest was going gray. Sander thought those symmetrical rows of muscle down his torso looked different. No longer did he look so much like he did sit-ups several hours a day. Now he looked like he needed to eat and keep on eating.

'What did your mother tell you?'

'How old you are.'

'She doesn't know how old I am.'

'I don't understand,' said Sander. 'Why would you keep that from me?'

'When you have a son, do it your own way.' He unbuttoned the shirt and took it from the hanger. 'I nearly waited too late to see you grow up, and that worried me for a while.'

'How old are you, dad?'

'But love isn't a thing you can rush. I don't think it even acknowledges time, you know? I'm glad you and Allie found each other when you did. I hope she's the one for you.'

'She is.'

'Hang on to her, then.' Dalton slid his arms into the shirt, then rolled his head in a great circle, his neck cracking in complaint or relief. He adjusted his collar. 'Did I ever tell you about Beau?'

'Beau who?'

Dalton sat in his dressing chair and leaned back. He blinked so slowly Sander thought he might go to sleep.

'Beau Grant. Bart's brother.'

'Bart had a brother? Granddad never said anything about it. I didn't know we could have brothers.'

'Your granddad tells you what I say he can tell you. It aint his fault. When your kid gets here, I won't say anything to him you don't want me to. Not about things like this.'

'I'll be able to talk to you, though, right?'

'Yes. But not to your granddad anymore. That's how it works. Anyway, that was the only time any of us could remember there being two boys. Hilda was an incredibly strong woman and Bart, for some reason, was small for a Grant. He weighed less than two stone when he was born and Hilda was hurt, but she healed. Beauregard was born two years later and looked just like his brother, only bigger.' He rubbed his forehead and closed his eyes for a long moment. 'I don't know, son. Maybe it was a bad idea. Maybe we shouldn't each have but one boy, no matter if we're able to have more. Beau and Bart didn't get along.'

'Do we ever have girls?'

'None that lived. I won't say it can't happen, but it hasn't in two centuries.' Getting back to his story, he said, 'It was like a competition, they say, always with the brothers. Beau ate more, worked harder, lifted things in his spare time. He willed himself to grow and it looked like it was working. When he got to nearly Bartholomew's size, their tussling turned to fighting. Awful fights. Augustus, their daddy, never would break it up. He believed they would see the foolishness of it soon enough. It would take care of itself. They wouldn't hurt one another, not really, he thought. But they did. Beau's aim was to knock his brother's block off so he could take his place. He wanted the ranch. At first, Bart was only trying to defend himself. That was easy when Beau was smaller. As his brother grew, Bart had to dig in and fight. It was vicious.' An afterthought occurred to Dalton and he said, 'Where's your mother?'

'In the kitchen.'

Dalton went on, 'Augustus still wouldn't stop the fights. The boys tore through the house and barn, smashing things up and knocking down walls. He made them take it outside, thinking, when one of them gets hurt bad enough, they'll stop. But we heal fast, son.'

Dalton pointed to the spot where the shovel had gashed him to the skull. The wound had already closed and looked almost superficial. He looked down and saw his own bloody knuckles had pushed out the bits of glass and they were mending.

'The brothers just got better at fighting,' said Dalton, 'better than anybody could know. Their father feared that another person might see them like that, see them turn like animals on one another.

'They would go to the thicket and have it out once or twice a month. There were a lot more hands on the ranch in those days. Riders to patrol the fence line and all. There wasn't machinery, so it took more help to run. These guys working here, they would see the treetops moving in the thicket. They would hear a roar and then a pounding wallop as one big pine swayed and bashed against another, limbs breaking. Then the brothers would come out all bloodied up, barely able to walk. You can imagine the talk around town.

'Nothing was ever settled between them. Beau would attack

his brother over the slightest thing. By the time Augustus figured he'd better put an end to it, it was too late. He found them in the thicket one day and knew right off he couldn't get between those boys and survive it. Already they were somehow stronger than him, meaner. Their eyes went a strange yellow and he had never heard such sounds come from a mouth. They swung logs at one another. They threw boulders and stumps trying to buy a breath, then one would fly pell-mell into his brother and pin him and pummel his face. They fought to kill. It horrified their father.'

'Jesus.'

'I know. He tried talking to his sons when things calmed down. First together, then separately. But each one swore he loved his brother. It didn't seem like they even remembered any of it. Like yard dogs drawing blood over a bone, then snuggling together under the house that night. It was more than Augustus could stand. His own father had warned him not to let his boys start fighting. He said that we were bred to do it, way back, and once we started, once we recalled that, we wouldn't stop. Augustus thought this was, I don't know, an old folktale or something. He didn't believe it until he saw it.'

'I'm having a hard time with it myself.'

'Well, believe it. Since he couldn't stand by and watch one son murder the other one, he decided the only thing to do was split them up. Beau, he reckoned, was more the troublemaker. He was restless, never content. So Augustus sent his youngest son away. He gave him money and some horses, but wouldn't give him any cattle. Never split the herd. His boy left the state and built him a small place up in Oklahoma where the land was cheaper. He would not see his family again. It hurt Augustus, but he thought he had fixed it where both his sons could have full lives. He was wrong. They both had a taste for it now. It was all Augustus could do to control Bart. The boy wanted to fight thunderheads. It took years to push that rage down where Bart could get hold of it, control it. Even then he was dangerous.

'And Beau, there was nobody to help him control anything. If he thought you looked at him cross, he'd push your house down. If somebody in town tried to raise their prices on supplies and he felt cheated? He'd find their field and kill their livestock one at a time, breaking their necks. You can imagine how well that went over. It didn't matter that the townspeople tried to leave him be. They had to deal with him, and they weren't gonna up and move away because of one person, giant or not. So they gathered up one night and went to Beau's place and shot him down. They burned his house, burned all his stuff, and put him in the ground.'

Dalton sat a short while and let that sink in. Then he got to the worst part.

'Word of it spread, but none of those people would mention the name Beau Grant after that. Like he never existed. Maybe they were able to forget about it up there, but not here. It was decades before anybody would deal directly with a Grant man again. When Augustus died, you can bet they kept a watchful eye on Bart for every hour of the day. They wouldn't let it get as bad here as it did up north. Your granddad was the first one of us they halfway trusted since all that happened. For the longest time, the women had to go into town alone and suffer the stares and muttering. Ranch hands had to buy all the supplies and bring them out. We were cheated and robbed all the time because we couldn't oversee our own affairs.'

'Shit.'

Dalton nodded. 'That's right. Do you see why I told you this?

Do you see why you can't do what you did today, why it scares me so?'

'No, sir. I mean, yes. Where in Oklahoma?'

'Washington County, I think. North of Tulsa.'

Sander was distracted for a moment, then asked, 'Do you hurt? You look like you hurt.'

'Naw. Just knocked the pride out of me. That's all. I'm fine. A little older, a little uglier, but I can still get the job done. A lot better than your mamma thinks, for sure. I kinda like her pampering me, though. Feels nice. I whine every once in a while. Gets me a back rub.'

'Feel like you could eat a bite?'

'Yeah.'

'I think it's ready. I'll meet you down there.'

Sander went straight for the Bible under his bed. He pulled out the news article and read it again. There was a driving atlas somewhere on his shelves. Finding it, he turned to the two-page spread on Oklahoma. Vera was a minuscule township about twenty-four miles north of Tulsa. A quarter of a century prior to the article's 1913 dateline would place the murder sometime around 1888. Beauregard would've been about four years older than Sander was now.

8

Though his father's cautionary tale about Beau gnawed at Sander, and the convoluted affairs of late robbed him of sleep for the second night in a row, he feared it might be days before he could get away from the ranch to have a long chat with Roger. That is, if Roger's offer stood which, after their last meeting, Sander had no way of guessing. However, when Spears' replacement, Miguel, arrived with Javier and Anthony, Sander was delighted to discover that the new guy had been, among other things, a carpenter. Rough framing was his specialty. And he brought his own tools. Things might go more smoothly than anticipated.

Sander first explained to his crew what needed doing today where the stock was concerned. Dalton took Anthony and the Smitherman brothers and they went to it, leaving Javier and Miguel awaiting instruction. Sander stood on the new concrete slab and started detailing how the walls of the meat cooler must be framed to allow for insulation, moisture barrier, drainage, and electrical.

Miguel listened politely until Sander paused, then said something in Spanish.

'He wants to know,' said Javier, 'do you have a drawing?'

'Well, no. I'm telling you how I want it.' Sander walked over to the stack of lumber and said, 'Here, I'll show you what I'm talking about,' and bent to pick up several two-by-sixes.

Miguel made a beckoning motion for Javier to speak.

'If you draw it, we can build it, Mr Sander. No problem.'

Sander thought about it. 'Alright. Come inside for a minute.'

Pinning McCoy's materials list to the top corner of his large sketch pad in the studio, Sander took his seat. With both men looking over his shoulder, he began to draw. He quickly laid out the entire structure, stick by stick, two different perspectives and three cross-sections. When he penciled in the door header, refrigeration support, and rafters, he tapped the materials list to indicate which boards were to be used.

'There's not much waste out there,' said Sander. 'We can't afford it.'

Javier translated to Miguel, then told Sander, 'We will need the roof decking day after tomorrow.'

'I think it's gonna take us a little longer than that,' Sander told them, as he rose and tore the drawing from the pad, 'but we'll see.'

Javier hesitated. 'It's a two-man job, Mr Sander. You have other stuff to do?'

'There's always other stuff to do, but this has to be done right.'

'*Sí, patrón*,' said Miguel. 'More better than these.' He took the drawing from Sander, rolled it and stuck it in his tool belt. '*Por si acaso.*'

'No problem,' Javier told Sander. 'Don't worry.'

Sander did worry, because Sander was a worrier. He poured a cup of coffee and spied on them from the kitchen while they positioned power tools, snapped some chalk lines and began cutting boards. In fifteen minutes, Sander determined these men knew more of carpentry than he cared to learn. Javier had put it more diplomatically than his brother-in-law but, in truth, Sander would've felt about as useful as tits on a boar out there and he doubted he could move fast enough to stay out of their way. This, he realized, was his chance to find Roger.

Sander parked on the gravel in front of First Unitarian. Roger stood on the porch sucking a Chesterfield. It was a repeat of their previous encounter, except there were no greetings this time.

'How did you know that was a relative of mine?' Sander asked. 'The skeleton in Oklahoma.'

'I didn't. Getting those people around Bartlesville to give up what they'd heard of the incident was like pulling crocodile teeth. It was a good guess, though. Your people seem to spread out. I've yet to read of two families of Nephilim within a thousand miles of one another. So there was a good chance he came from here.'

'I see,' said Sander. 'Do you feel like telling me what or who Nephilim is?'

'Sure.' Roger thumped his cigarette at the exact moment a gust of wind came and the butt traveled an impossible distance across the lawn to ricochet off the head of the propane tank in a shower of sparks. Roger either didn't notice, or didn't care. 'Come on in. Watch your head on the stairs.' He led Sander up to his private study and closed the door behind them.

'Please,' he told his guest, 'get as comfortable as you can on that sofa. I'm sorry I don't have anything bigger.' Sander did, while Roger produced a decanter of wine and held it up to the shafts of sunlight coming through the blinds.

'Thanks,' said Sander, 'but I don't drink in the morning.'

Roger chuckled. 'I wouldn't have taken you for a drinker at all.

A good thing, because I don't have enough for two. I was checking to see if there was anything growing in it. It's cheap and it's old. Scares me a little.' He added, 'Thanks for pointing out the hour, though.'

He poured a water glass full of the stuff and searched through a lopsided pile on his desk, pulling out several pieces of paper. He gulped some wine and began scouring a bookshelf to the left of the window.

'Nephilim?' Sander reminded him.

'That's you. Your kind. One of the words the Israelites had for you, anyway. I didn't mean to mystify you with it.' Sander thought otherwise. Roger turned and flung a small, tattered volume in his lap. 'You read the King James, I'm guessing. That,' he pointed to the little book, 'is a translation of the Hebrew text before Christians went to work on it. Not hard to find.' Roger was searching for something else. 'You're familiar with Genesis 6, verse 4.' It wasn't a question. 'Have a look at it in that version. Page 12.'

Sander read:

> The Nephilim were on the earth in those days – and also afterward – when the sons of God went in to the daughters of humans, who bore children to them. These were the heroes that were of old, warriors of renown.

No sooner had he finished, than Roger tossed him another.

'The Matthew's Bible. First one authorized in English, about seventy-five years before the King James. Think of it as King Henry the Eighth's version.' Sander didn't open it. 'Go ahead,' said Roger, 'see what Henry's guys called you.'

> There were tyrants in the world in those days. For after that the children of God had gone in unto the daughters of men –

Sander closed the book. Roger had gathered what he sought. He sat with his armload in the chair across the coffee table from Sander and glanced at his glass of wine on the desk.

'Yeah,' said Roger. 'In less than a century, you went from tyrants to giants. Long before that, heroes and warriors. You went back to Nephilim in the 1800s with the English Revised Version, roughly the same time "children of God" was taken to mean angels. But you were never heroes again. Officially. I'm sure you've seen the way you're characterized in later passages. Not flattering.'

Sander was suddenly incensed. The fact that he couldn't get a firm handle on the reason for his anger did little to quell it. Something in the authority with which Roger spoke of the Grant heritage. As it might be, Sander imagined, for a midget listening to Tolkien talk of hobbits like they walked Dixon streets. More, though, there was an undercurrent working in Sander's mind. He was at last fitting together the pieces from recent events.

'So you go around stalking big people until you can convince one that he's some kind of ... what? I think you came here looking for us. You found out about Jason. Made him your little spy and now mamma's taking the blame on herself.'

'You had the talk with your mother, didn't you?'

'She told me God said not to come here. Starting to sound like a wise move.'

'He said more than that.' Roger stacked his books and papers on the table between them. 'I understand why she's upset. I've been warned before and it's never easy. Never pleasant.'

'Warned?'

'Yeah. Except this time – and I'm assuming Josephine got the same treatment I did – this time it was more of a threat. That can rattle a person, even a strong one.'

'Okay, Roger.' Sander closed his eyes, hoping that when he opened them there wouldn't be a lunatic sitting over there. No such luck. 'God's threatening you now?'

'And you, your family. More yall than me, actually. He just refuses to talk to you.'

'Lookit, I'm gonna head on back to the ranch,' Sander said, hands on his knees, 'and if God aint smote it with locusts or frogs, I intend to get some work done. I'm tempted to suggest you see somebody about this stuff, maybe get yourself a little medication, but I reckon I'll stay the hell out of your business. From now on, I need you to do me the same favor. That goes for Jason too, if you happen to see him. We clear?'

'You never told Jason that you speak to your dead relatives, did you? Or, more to the point, that they speak back.'

'Do what?'

'I didn't think so. Wouldn't reflect favorably on your state of mind.' Roger was much more afraid of Sander's temper than he evidenced, but he had to do something to keep him here. 'I don't deny stalking giants. Stalk is a good word for it. You can scarcely imagine how many cases of Marfan syndrome, Sotos syndrome, hypergonadism and various thyroid tumors I've seen or studied. Each of them resulting in what's crudely termed gigantism.' He laughed at himself. 'All those semesters I spent with the rock hounds in the archaeology department ... Look,' he said, extending several stapled pieces of paper, the top one crammed with his handwriting. Sander didn't move.

'I didn't give you that newspaper article because it was the only one I could find,' said Roger. He read from stapled sheets, 'The *Semi-Weekly Cedar Falls Gazette*, September of 1897. The *Fort Wayne News* out of Indiana. That one was January, 1901. And,' he flipped over two pages, 'closer to home we've got the *San Antonio Express* from April of 1931 and the *Amarillo Globe-Times*. Sure you don't wanna have a look?' He met Sander's stare. 'Alright. In January, that last one will be only thirty years old. Every one of these is an article about the remains of giants. Unearthed accidentally, and now they're in a museum somewhere. There's better than sixty articles here.' He placed the pages on the coffee table. 'Don't take my word for it, though. The library can get you copies of all the American ones.'

'That's good to know.'

'Maybe it doesn't interest you. It evidently doesn't interest too many people. You're not as newsworthy as you were at the turn of the century. Anyway, some of the bones they've dug up are ancient. Some not so much. I've seen them all. From France, to India, to Scotland. Despite what's been written about your family over the years – and there hasn't been much – you already know you don't have any hormonal or thyroid condition.' Sander had no reaction, but Roger knew he was right. 'Such things are never consistent in an unbroken lineage and, at any rate, fail to account for your strength, your intellectual development, and the fact that you can speak with the dead.'

'After all these years,' Sander said, 'here comes an over-educated preacher who can explain it all for us. Our forefathers were angels. Now it makes perfect sense.'

'Not perfect, but a good deal of sense. I understand why you're looking at me like that. I must seem like one of those Sasquatch hunters with all my "documented sightings". I would hope–'

'That's not funny,' said Sander.

'No. It isn't. A single thing, if nothing else, separates me from those people and the folks searching the sky for UFOs: I'm sitting across from a giant.' Roger curtailed that thread and confessed, 'I've been pursuing the truth behind scripture for thirty years, Sander, since my first undergraduate course in biblical history. I'm still not sure who the "children of God" are, but I intend to find out. Yes, it is an obsession.' He added, 'It's not limited to Nephilim, either. If I'm wrong in the head, then I'm way more nuts than you think.'

'What makes you think we talk to the dead?'

'It was written once about your people. Specifically one named Bilgames. You probably know him as Gilgamesh. I have the original cuneiform if you'd like to see it.'

'When I first came here, you mentioned helping me. That's not your aim with this.'

'Yes it is, albeit secondarily. Sincere, though.'

'Secondary to what?'

'A restoration.' He held up the two Bibles from the coffee table. 'What baffles the best of us, scholars of these writings, is how they sold this stuff to begin with. As much *hoodoo* as it seems now, Greek mythology makes more sense than the words we hold sacred. A whole heap less paradoxical, anyway. The simplest ancient Sumerian wouldn't have accepted this text, not like it stands today. Not as it has been for a millennium. So, what did they accept? What did they buy into?' He plopped the books back on the table. 'It very nearly starts with the Nephilim. Your kind were living proof to the veracity of the gospel. Proof is something the Olympians couldn't offer. The origin of your people is woven into the backstory of divine creation, the monotheistic version. That's what I mean when I say I can help you. I can help you know who you are.' Roger leaned forward in his chair.

'Do you remember my talk on Noah and the flood? Or, forget my talk, you know the tale. God made a point of sparing the seed of mankind along with all the other animals which couldn't swim or fly. Except Nephilim. The King James tells us God said to Noah, "And of every living thing of all flesh, two of every sort shalt thou bring into the ark," and so forth. But that's not how the Hebrew translates. More accurately, it says "all *natural* flesh". The Talmud – Rabbinic writings, Jewish, fifth century – it says your people survived because one of you clung to the hull of the ark. Imagine it. The torrent comes without warning and you're left to drown. For forty days, nine hundred and sixty hours, you hold fast, hand gripping that gopher wood like a vice, struggling to fill your lungs between swells.' He snapped out of his admiration and appended an afterthought. 'But why forty days? That's the question nobody's asking. I mean, how long can an average human being tread water, you reckon? No, God was serious about killing, and the animal He set out to kill was very strong. The rest of the poor sinners who went under were, foremost, collateral damage. Made for a good lesson on divine wrath, though.'

Roger had allowed his fervor to get the better of his propriety. He was thankful Sander wasn't headed for the door.

'Let me ask you something,' said Sander. 'Do you believe in God? Wait. Stupid question. Of course you do. He talks to you and all. I mean to say, do you believe He is the Creator, or do you just study Him like a historian might dig into the life of Plato or Aristotle?'

'Both. One without the other would seem foolish to me. Interesting that you should bring up Aristotle.' He began thumbing through his stack of material. 'He actually wrote of the beginning. I have it here somewhere.'

'Don't bother. Can God hear us right now?'

'Oh, you betcha,' answered Roger, without looking up.

'And His warning or threat to you evidently concerns what we're talking about.'

'God's monarchy is not absolute, Sander. He's ultimately accountable–' Roger thought he found what he was looking for. As he scanned the page, from force of habit he lapsed into his teaching mode and was saying, 'You didn't believe Aristotle invented oligarchy, did you? He named it, so we're told, but there has always been a council, or governing body, behind the scenes in heaven. Read these few–'

When Roger did look up, extending pages once again, Sander was walking past him.

'Where you going?'

Sander turned, his hand on the doorknob. 'Roger, I think you've got a screw loose. If not, we're sitting around pissing off the Almighty while you drink spoiled wine. Either way, it doesn't seem like a good way to spend the morning, does it?' Sander ducked under the doorway and headed down the stairs.

Roger called after him, 'Maybe a little of both! It's worth finding out what He said to your mom, though!'

Sander pulled into the ranch drive and was astounded to see two stud walls standing on the concrete slab out back. Javier was helping Miguel assemble a third. He parked the truck and had his hand on the gate when he looked to his left.

Jo was on her knees in the backyard, buckled at the waist with her forehead resting in a brown patch of St Augustine grass. Sander cut and ran over to her. As he drew closer, he heard her slow sobbing.

Miguel stopped hammering and looked their way. Javier scolded him in Spanish and they both returned to their work.

'Mamma, what's wrong?'

Jo didn't seem to notice him there. Instinctively, he put his big hands on her shoulders and tried to coax her up. He moved her an inch and thunder punched the ground, bouncing lawn chairs on the patio and rattling the corrugated barn roof. There wasn't a cloud in the sky. Jo wailed and arched her back as though something had seized the base of her spine and snatched it downward. The sound she made was that of a cornered panther; of pain so near madness that there was no difference. Sander saw her face and, for an instant, did not recognize her. He had to stop himself from recoiling. Her head returned to the earth and the sobbing continued.

'Don't touch her,' called Dalton from the patio door. He held the phone receiver to his chest, the cord stretched to its breaking point.

No good. Sander couldn't help it. He was already bent to scoop his mother from the ground. Again, at the tiniest movement, thunder slammed the land from all directions. This one knocked spit from Sander's open mouth.

Jo loosed another primal squall, Sander released her, and she mumbled, 'I'm not. Not moving.' At least, that's what Sander thought she said. Her blistering scream had his ears ringing and he couldn't be sure. Her head fell back where it was.

'Goddamnit, son.' Dalton shoved Sander on his rump. 'I told you to leave her be.' Then, to Jo, 'The ambulance is on its way, honey.'

Not too many places you can lay the blame for inexplicably punctual thunder. Looking up at the blue sky, Sander could think of only one. As the three of them sat in the yard awaiting the paramedics, he was not altogether surprised when the pain left Jo's body as mysteriously as it had stricken her. Nor was he taken aback by his mother's attitude toward the ordeal. At the hospital, while a nurse drew vials of her blood, Jo was resigned to the inconvenience, like she was waiting on a dim-witted trainee at the supermarket to figure out the cash register. Dalton was utterly distraught, however, and that tested Jo's patience, so she sent him in search of ginger ale.

When the nurse left the room, Sander said, 'What do you think it was?'

'I don't have to think. He told me.'

'God talked to you while you were hurting?'

'Yes.'

'What did He say?'

'He said be still. He just wanted you to see it, then He said it would go away. It did.'

'Why would He do that?'

Jo heard boot heels on the linoleum in the hall. 'Let's talk about it later.'

The doctor said Jo's blood work would take twenty-four hours. He made his prediction that it was just a pinched nerve, sent Jo home with a sample of anti-inflammatory drugs and prescribed rest until the labs came back. Dalton put her to bed and joined Sander on the sofa in the living room.

'I sent everybody home,' said Sander.

'Good. That's good. I'm worried that something is bad wrong with her.'

'Don't be, dad. I think the doctor is right. Something got twisted or pinched. I bet it's nothing serious.'

'Have you ever seen a person hurt like that?'

'I have now.' He rose and grabbed his truck keys off the table. 'That medicine is gonna knock her out for a while. I need to run back over to the church. I forgot something.'

'Bring back dinner,' said Dalton.

Sander was pounding on the church door fifteen minutes later. Roger hurried down the stairs to unlock it before the thing flew from its hinges.

'What's wrong?'

'The threat,' Sander blurted. 'What did God say?'

Roger invited him in and they stood in the back of the dark meeting hall.

'In essence,' Roger told him, 'He said leave well enough alone. He got kind of archaic with the "or else" part. Lots of "thee" and "thine" and verbs ending with e-t-h. He does that when He's hiding something.'

'Leave what alone?'

'I told you I've been working on biblical translations, restoring lost and distorted scripture. I've had a modicum of success over the years, all things considered. Some of the stuff that was originally there – God wasn't too happy to see it in print in the first place. Nothing to be done about it, though. Man wrote it and it was factual. His council would have been eager to remind him of that.' Which explained a sum total of nothing for Sander. Roger said, 'It seems the Nephilim might be a particularly sore subject for the Almighty.'

'Okay. Back up. You keep saying these things as if God has no choice in the matter. What council are you talking about?'

'See, it was a stroke of luck for God that man started revising the *Word*. For the most part, we took out or changed the parts He didn't like. Now there's just enough truth left to impress the faithful and the rest of it makes any questions look argumentative, at best. But just as we were the only ones who could change it, we're also the only ones who can change it back. I know it doesn't make a whole lot of sense right now, sort of disjointed. I need to run up and get a few of those items you didn't see before you left.' Yet he made no move to get up. Instead, he asked, 'Why the change of heart?'

Sander told him the story, in brief.

Roger shook his head.

'I was hoping that it wouldn't come to that, but it makes sense that He used her.'

'She didn't do anything. Why not hurt you?' Sander said. 'You started it.'

'True enough, in a manner of speaking. But you don't care one way or another for me. Much more effective to use Josephine. If He stops you, then He's stopped me. On the Nephilim front, at least.' Roger studied Sander for a moment. 'And He has stopped you, hasn't He?'

'I guess He has, yeah. I'm not really sure I was on board to begin with.'

'That's His way. Very proactive, most of the time.'

'Then, why didn't He come to me? Warn me?'

'God can't lay a finger on you, kid. The Nephilim belong to the holy council and it's strictly hands-off for Jehovah. Has been for quite some time. I'm still working on the details of that.' Standing, he said, 'I made you some copies, so you might as well take them. I'll just be a minute. Help yourself to the coffee.'

Sander was coming out of the kitchen when he heard Roger trotting back down the stairs, mumbling something that seemed to make him chuckle. When he reached the bottom step, he collapsed to his knees on the hardwood and all he carried flew asunder before him. He grabbed his head with both hands. Sander had seen this pose before, like the man was being pressed to the ground by the nape of his neck. Sander rushed over, but knew better than to touch him.

'What's He saying?' asked Sander. 'I'll leave.' Roger made no sound, his hands white against his temples. 'Should I leave?' Sander whispered.

Roger struggled to get out one word, 'Wait.'

Sander watched Roger lower his forehead back to the floor and breathe deliberately until he could speak again.

'Medicine in the kitchen,' he managed.

Sander had noticed it by the coffee maker, a little brown bottle labeled 'Roxanol Oral'. He fetched it.

Lips against the plank floor, Roger said, 'Take the top off.' Then, very slowly, he raised his head enough to drink.

'Your nose is bleeding,' said Sander. 'Pretty bad.'

'It'll stop.'

Sander recapped the bottle. Roger clamped his head between his hands again, not as tightly this time. His muscles gradually relaxed. Blood trickled between his wrists. Sander went for a roll of paper towels.

In a short while, Roger was able to get himself upright and into the lavatory. He cleaned his face and reemerged a few minutes later. Sander had wiped up the blood and stacked Roger's papers on the pew. They sat on either side of the stack and Sander handed over the medicine bottle. Roger shook it, then slid it into his pocket.

'He's got all His toys out at your place,' said Roger. Balled-up toilet tissue corked each nostril, making his voice nasal. 'Thunder, wind, fire, the whole show. It wouldn't do for people to see the wrath of God coming down in church, so He hits me quietly. A little tumor to keep me humble.'

'Roger, I'm sorry.'

'Don't worry about it.' He patted his pocket. 'Morphine. Life's full of tradeoffs.'

'What's He pissed at now?' asked Sander.

'This,' said Roger, pointing to the stack between them. 'If you want the knowledge, it's your right to have it. Your right to understand.' A shard of pain cut through the dense curtain of narcotic. Roger tensed, then relaxed. 'Take it with you and read it.'

'You're saying get out?'

'I'm saying it looks like I have to listen to Him for now. I'm not sorry for what I've done, only for what happened because of it. I'll pray for your mother.'

Sander wondered how much of it was the drug talking. 'So, how am I supposed to feel toward God?'

'Honestly, I've thought about it a good bit from your perspective. Or I've tried.' Roger closed his eyes to concentrate when his speech started to slur. 'God didn't make the Nephilim and for a very long time He's chosen to have nothing to do with your kind. He can act like a petulant kid sometimes, but His heart is good. He's my Father, my absolution, my Alpha and Omega. I need to love Him.' He corrected himself, 'I need Him and I love Him. I believe He loves me. I don't know what to tell you to believe, Sander.' Then, opening his eyes, 'You don't smoke, do you?'

'No.'

'Crap.'

Roger made his way up the stairs, stopping to steady himself on each one.

Surely he's in a stupor now, thought Sander, as he listened to Roger trail off, '... because heaven *doesn't* presuppose hell, any more than it means we'll ever see either place. I so envy your afterlife. So sinfully covet ...'

Sander turned off the lights and locked the door when he left.

9

Sander was in no great hurry to read the pages scattered in the truck seat beside him. He hadn't really wanted to take them from the church, fearing what might befall Roger – or worse, his mother – if he did. Yet Roger had offered them when it looked reasonably certain he had one foot in the grave and the other on a slick spot. It would've been rude to leave them. The damage was done, anyway, and he had already stated he had no intention of helping Roger sift through his ancient writings to reconstruct the gospel. Was reconstruct the word Roger used? Sander told himself he would toss all the pages in the garbage when he got home. After he read them.

Once on his way, he realized home seemed less like a haven and more like a battleground now. Sander first wondered whose fault that was, then asked himself whether blame made any difference. He had always revered the truth of things and summarily concluded that he would rather not feel safe if safety was an illusion. Which thought led him to another, regarding knowledge in general.

Surely, in thirty years, Roger had tracked down every scrap

of information on Nephilim. Sander was momentarily distracted, trying to get used to that word, as applied to himself, his kin. It felt more natural each time he heard it in his head. He said it aloud a couple of times. Yes, better than when Roger said it. When Sander snapped out of his digression, he returned to the subject of Roger's purpose. If the man had compiled all the available literature on giants, and if he believed what he read, what use was a live one, other than a curious talking exhibit?

Roger wasn't like that. He had nothing to prove and nobody to impress and – Sander stopped, mid-thought – and *he didn't want a live one*. He wanted to talk to the dead ones. That's the point they hadn't reached. Roger was a historian. He wanted Sander to help him fill in the holes in his research by talking to Will. Sander was convinced. More specifically, Roger wanted to hear, through Will, what the older ones might have to say.

Sander could've kicked himself. Of course God wouldn't get so worked up over stuff virtually anybody could find in the dusty stacks of some university library. If it was archived, it was available. Because He knew Roger's mind, God was several steps ahead of that. If Roger was right, God adamantly objected to Sander resurrecting things that were no longer written record; things, if he went back far enough, his ancestors would doubtless remember firsthand. His grandfather had told him that other clans, distant ancestors, were 'hard to find'. Hard. Not impossible.

It was going on seventy-two hours now since Sander had slept, but the need to talk trumped his body's call for rest. His mother would be asleep. If she wasn't, she should be, and Sander was not inclined to revisit the subject with her until he'd had time to work it out a bit further for himself. Moreover, he determined that if his dad lived out the rest of his days and never had to deal with this colossal bullshit, that would suit him fine. Dalton had enough on his mind.

Sander stopped at the next gas station to use the payphone.

'¡*Hola*!' said Clarita.

'Mrs Sandoval, can I speak to Allie?'

'It's late, Sander.'

'I know, ma'am.'

'And it's a school night.'

'Yes, ma'am, but it's very important.'

Sander heard the receiver hit the counter, then voices in the background.

'Hello?' Allie said.

'I'm coming over. I need to talk.'

'Hurry,' she said. 'Papa's at the store. He'll be back any minute.'

Allie was standing out in the drive when he pulled up. She jumped into the truck and said, 'Let's take a drive.' He shifted into reverse. 'What's this?' she asked, pulling the papers from under her.

'Nothing,' said Sander. He stuffed them behind the seat.

'How's your mom?'

'You heard?'

'Somebody said something at the store. It's the only reason mamma let me out this late.'

'She's fine. A pinched nerve, they think. Can you ride with me to pick up some burgers for dad?'

'Sure. I've got about an hour.'

'I don't. He'll start eating raw meat if I'm not back soon.' Allie laughed. He asked her, 'Do you love me?'

'You know I do.'

Sander turned onto the highway, headed toward town. 'Then marry me.'

'Okay,' she said. 'I think the courthouse closes at five, but we might could squeeze it in between school and work tomorrow.'

'I'm serious. Not this week, but maybe this coming summer.'

She turned in her seat to face him. 'You're crazy. I'm sixteen!'

'But you'll be seventeen in July.'

'Have you been drinking?'

'People talk about my family, and I'm sure you've heard it. I've got forty-five good years and I don't feel like waiting for some arbitrary age to get married when I know what I want right now. I can explain this to Jaime where he'll understand.'

'Can you? Then explain it to me. Tell me how you've thought about what I want. How it affects me.'

'I'm asking you now what you want, Allie. Do you want to marry me?'

She turned forward again and latched her seatbelt. 'Next time, save me some booze. I thought we were supposed to go to a movie the other night.' They rode in silence for a mile. 'Okay,' she said, 'here's what I want. Onions. Lots of em. Two slices of cheese and no tomatoes. I hate tomatoes.'

'Whatever,' said Sander. 'You think your mom and dad would like a burger too?'

'Thanks, but they're having *menudo*. Tripe is something else I can't stand. Think you can remember that? Tomatoes and tripe?'

Sander was parking in front of the Dairy Queen. 'Back in a second,' he said.

She grabbed his arm. 'Because, if you can, and if you can convince papa, I'll marry you whenever you want, babe.'

'Really?'

'Yeah. I wouldn't suggest you mention dying at forty-five. Tell him how good the ranch is doing.' With a grand gesture, she added, 'His daughter's life will be free of worry and his grandson will be raised a Catholic. That's a good start.'

She was genuine in her sentiment, thought Sander – only, she reckoned stars would dance while the moon played a jig before her father would agree to any wedding. Sander was glad, in a way, that she used Jaime as such a device, forestalling her own commitment until it comfortably fit her, as it might have done immediately if he had been capable of making more clear the love behind his offer, instead of relying on the logic of it. Ten percent laziness, he decided, and ninety percent his own ineptitude at things like this.

Dalton was asleep in his chair in front of the television when Sander walked in. He put the sacks of food on the table and gently shook his dad's shoulder.

'Food,' he said.

They discussed the next day's work in choppy sentences while they ate. Neither had their usual appetite.

Jo stopped taking her pills the next day. She was back to her chores long before the hospital called that afternoon. The blood work was normal, they said, and she was to return to the ER immediately if the pain recurred. She didn't make it three steps toward the laundry room before the phone was ringing again. This time it was Jason.

'Mrs Grant,' he said, 'you're up and around?'

'I'm fine, Jason. Seems the whole town was worried and it was just a little catch in my back. Nothing, really. You want to talk to Sander?'

'Yes, ma'am, if he's nearby.'

'He's out at the barn. I'll holler for him.'

Jo wasn't there to tell Sander who was on the other end of the line when he walked in.

'Sander Grant,' he said into the receiver.

'Did you hear from Roger?'

Damn, thought Sander, his mom could've guessed this call wasn't worth interrupting his afternoon. 'Not lately,' Sander lied. 'Why?'

'He called everybody in the congregation. Cancelled this Sunday's service. Said he wasn't feeling well, that's it. I came home to the message on my machine.'

'The flu. It's going around.'

'Kinda odd,' Jason ventured, 'that he didn't call you too.'

There might have been a touch of suspicion in his voice, and it might have been Sander's imagination. Whatever the case, he had diesel fuel all over him, he was running behind, and in no mood to chitchat. He was seeing Allie again early this evening, and the evening after that, and the evening after that, until they agreed upon a game plan for approaching Jaime about getting hitched. He bore no ill will toward Roger, but already knew what was ailing him and Sander wanted the man out of his mind for a while.

'I reckon he figured you would tell me. Is that all you called for, Jason? I'm pretty busy.'

'Well, no, actually. I spoke with Scott Jacob yesterday. He's awfully anxious for another piece from you.'

'He didn't call me either. Doesn't matter, though. I don't have anything for him. I was meaning to talk to you before next week anyhow. I'm not painting at all these days so we need to hold off on the lessons.'

'For how long?' asked Jason.

'Until further notice.'

'Not the lessons. Screw the lessons. How long do you intend to let your talent lie dormant? It won't wait on you forever. Neither will your patrons.'

'Until further notice,' Sander repeated. 'When you see Roger, tell him I hope he gets to feeling better.'

'You're quitting the church, too?'

'I was never a member of your church. Thanks for having me out to visit, but I don't think I'll be coming around anymore. Take it easy.'

'Can I–'

Sander hung the receiver back on the wall. He liked the way he had stumbled onto a sort of Dalton-esque method of handling his affairs. He managed to dismiss Jason in under a minute, while simultaneously sending his farewell, via the grapevine, to Dixon's religious community. The approach worked – to get things started, anyway – when he proposed to Allie last night, too. Straightforward, well considered, and absent varnish. He recalled how he'd convinced Dalton himself to buy feed from the Sandovals and he realized his dad's modus operandi had served him for some time now, when he let it. Stop juggling decisions like some masochistic circus clown, he told himself. Vital or trivial, confront the thing and act.

'You gonna stare out that window all day or get back to work?' Jo asked, as she dumped the laundry basket onto the table and began folding.

Sander blurted, 'I'm done with church, mamma, but I'm tired of pussyfooting around the subject of God, me and you. We both know He struck you down in the yard with some affliction even the doctors can't find, and for reasons unclear to me, we're keeping that from dad. I wanna know what God said to you. His words.'

'Do you?' The expression on her face when she whirled on him caused Sander to reconsider this tack when it came to his mother. She was no stranger to it and responded in kind. 'Alright, let's see.' Jo glanced up, as though the words hung in the air above her. '"For the sake of My name I delay My wrath, and for My praise I restrain it for you, in order not to cut you off."'

'Mom, that's the Bible. I don't know which verse, but He's quoting the book of Isaiah. Are you sure He said that?' Didn't appear to Sander at the time that any wrath was delayed. Then again, she wasn't bleeding from the face and swilling morphine yet, either.

'I know where it comes from.'

'Seems like he could get some new material, is all.'

'He also said that I would suffer only until you witnessed it, then it would go away. That's the part He wanted me to tell you, and I did. You know, it felt like hours until you drove up. Dalton said it was just a few minutes.' She waited for the memory of the pain and fear to release her, then said flatly, 'I will not forgive you if you tell your father it was your fault.' Then, indicating the unfinished chore behind her, 'Was there anything else?'

'Yeah. Do you know what it was all about?'

'I'm not stupid, son. And I'm not saying it's right, or that it's fair. I've learned to let fairness work itself out in the bigger picture. You keep doing what you feel like you need to do. I mean that. I couldn't tolerate it any other way. Only, now you know the consequences. I reckon that was God's point,' she said, 'but I could be wrong. Nothing's stopping you from talking to Him about it.'

'I don't have one-sided conversations. It's pointless.'

'Hmm,' Jo grunted, barely audible. She returned to her laundry, leaving her son standing there with his stony mask. She would not debate with him the legitimacy of prayer. That argument was for children and philosophers.

Sander had long considered 'fairness in the big picture' and many another grand-scheme-of-things viewpoint as the strategy of an ostrich. If there was an equitable grand scheme, then somewhere down the line there must be a reconciliation. The books should balance. Therefore, when innocent people are beleaguered and the weaker man takes one on the chin for the sake of the stronger, it must mean that elsewhere a fool is rewarded for the work of wise men and the like. He was old enough to know that occasionally this happened, but should it be accepted as ordained? Should it be ignored at the highest level, he wondered.

Indeed, his mother was not stupid. Nor was Roger. Both, in distinct ways, were the smartest people he had come across; both confident in what they knew. They had something else in common. They shared a voluntary selectiveness of sight that allowed for a level of conviction beyond faith – which was a term, through his experience in the town's churches, Sander had learned to translate as hope. All hope is subject at some point to validation. Not so with Jo and Roger. Theirs was a strength insusceptible to trial. Sander recalled Roger's drug-induced mumbling and now found it difficult to control his own envy. Maybe, if he could have a single exchange with God, no matter how cryptic, he could find such powerful belief and manage to hang onto it.

'How come you can hear Him and I can't?' he asked, 'that's what bugs me.'

Over her shoulder, Jo said, 'Maybe for the same reason He can hurt me, but can't lay a hand on you.'

'How did you–'

'If He could make you feel what I did out there on the grass, we wouldn't be having this discussion. Now get out of here. My sheets are starting to smell like a grease pit.'

Sander and Allie talked so much about different ways of approaching her father, different times of day and days of the week versus others, that the scenario inevitably became hypothetical. Early on, in way of concession to her dread over D-day, and to nudge her closer to believing the thing would happen sooner than later, Sander had guaranteed her that he wouldn't cross the line and even hint at marriage near Jaime before they were both ready. He failed to foresee how such a compromise would negate his newfound head-on way of solving problems. Now he was starting to resent Allie for her indecision. Their discussions about it first fell away from nightly to biweekly, then weekly, and ultimately occurred only when Sander was perturbed about something else and needed to vent. Her procrastination was an easy target, and his tendency to harp on it ruined Christmas between them.

When Sander awoke on the first of January and tore December's page from his wall calendar, several thoughts bombarded him in succession. Written there in the square of the fourteenth was 'Argos'. To make this season's market list with the distribution company, that date absolutely could not be pushed out farther. The cooler was finished and ready, but the slaughterhouse, which they had been relegated to constructing with reclaimed and below-grade materials, was three-quarters done, at best. Thirteen days, thought Sander, and he berated himself for giving his men both New Year's Eve and New Year's Day off. Grant Beef was not a department store and couldn't, especially now, afford this down time.

Next thing to hit him concerned the wadded calendar page in his hand. He tried to remember how many of these he had tossed in the waste basket since he proposed to Allie. How many since he talked to his mom about God and resolved absolutely nothing? At least a fiscal quarter had gone down in the ranch books since he promised himself he would, first thing tomorrow, visit the hill by the pond. Tomorrows kept coming and he gave a wide berth to that inconspicuous spot in the back field.

He stared at the captioned heading atop the remaining page in the spiral binding on his wall.

> Make 1990 Your Best Year Yet!
> Visit your local True Value for a new calendar & great deals to start off right.

This was the first year Sander could remember that he did not feel prepared to handle from the outset. Despite what he had been telling himself of late, all about marching headlong through doubt and taking challenges in hand, he realized that he had steered his attention toward the easier problems and left the rest for another day. Was that day on the last page of this calendar, he asked himself, or was it buried deep in the next?

The Smitherman brothers had taken care of the needs of the herd for a couple of days, and Dalton would be checking the pastures periodically. Anthony had stacked every available scrap of building material in sorted piles near the slaughterhouse site. After seeing what Javier and Miguel made of his plans for the meat cooler, Sander dared not meddle with whatever system they had underway thereabouts. Other than black-eyed peas and cabbage with his folks at lunch and, later, tamales with Allie and her family, his slate was clear for the day. As Jo cleaned the breakfast dishes,

Sander announced that he was going to visit his grandfather and might be a while.

'Tell him I'll be up there this afternoon,' said Dalton.

It was cold out and the wind had a razor's edge that cut wool and cotton alike. Sander decided to drive a half mile of the way and walk the rest. When he parked, he saw the breeding stock of the middle field slowly converging on his truck. They would discover soon enough that he wasn't there with new mineral licks and they would disperse again to their hay feeders and shelters. The sky was a chalky slate from edge to edge and threatened snow.

He tilted up his seat and reached into the back of the cab for a canvas tarpaulin and a couple of saddle blankets. His hand found Roger's crumpled copies. Sander had read them, piecemeal, skipping some here and there for time's sake. He paid close enough attention to all the highlighted parts, then he literally put the stuff behind him. The pages were stained now, with everything from chain rust to Cheetos dust, but they were legible. Sander evened up the stack, folded it and tucked it in his back pocket to get it out of the way.

On the hill, he made a nest against the oak; canvas beneath him to shield against the frozen grass, and he laid the saddle blankets over his legs.

'Cold out here, granddad.' Sander shivered.

'Oh,' said Will, 'you'll survive. We were beginning to doubt there'd be enough frost to kill the mosquitoes this year. So pleasant since October, and all.'

'Yeah. I haven't been up in a while. Sorry.'

'No need, Sander. I've told you how time passes for us. Seconds to the day, if that. We're not sitting around pining for company.'

Sander wasn't sure if his grandfather was stretching the truth for his benefit. No way to know, he guessed, until he rested under this tree.

'Reckon dad's told you how well the ranch is doing.'

'He aint exactly been a font of information, worried as he is. But, yeah, he gave us the herd numbers. Says the place is turning into a regular compound up near the house. Says you're responsible for all that.'

'Worried about what?' Sander asked.

'Your mom. You.'

'Did he tell you last quarter was the most profitable in our history, and that the meat distributor is coming this month?'

A sibilant sound emanated from the ground and Sander thought his granddad might be sucking his teeth or chewing on a sourweed root.

'That's great, son,' said Will. 'You're aware, though, that there are things more important than this ranch, right? Cause, if not, you have no business running it.'

'Mom's fine. Right as the rain. I can't imagine why dad would be worried about me.'

'Got us thinking,' said Will, and Sander could tell by the change in tone that somebody else, Jed maybe, was bending his ear. 'You'd be surprised at how some of us acted when we first heard voices in the sod. My daddy brung me up here to talk with Bart and all I could think to do was test him, like you would a two-bit magician at the carnival. Had this old pair of horseshoe pull-offs in my coat and I hid em behind my back. "What's in my hand?" I said. He didn't cotton to it, but I clammed up and pouted until he played along. He got it on the first guess. Pretty impressive, to a kid. He made a believer out of me.'

'It's gonna snow soon, granddad, and there's something I wanted to talk to you about.'

Will ignored him. 'Anyway, lots of funny stories like that and I don't mind telling on myself. Then there's this other story. Goes like this. A kid comes up here and hears the voice of his deceased grandfather and asks, "Can you talk to others that aint buried here?" Now, being as we were all in your shoes at one time, we're fairly accustomed to questions. That one, though, it seems a little far-fetched coming right out of the gate, wouldn't you say?

'But we all want to thank you, Sander. Since you started us along that road, we've been talking to people we had only heard stories about. Augustus hasn't spoken with his grandee Liam since the Spanish left the territory. Turns out somebody moved his grave. He's buried up in Missouri beside Moses Austin himself. Aint that something! I didn't know we knew the Austins. That was just the beginning, too. We've gone back way further than that.'

'Yeah. I want to hear about it. Thing is –'

'Couldn't find Beauregard, though. Bart really wanted to talk to his brother. Lot of things left unsaid there.'

'Dad told me about all that.'

'Yeah.'

'They dug him up, granddad,' said Sander, an inkling settling upon him that Will might be going somewhere with this. 'Beau. His skeleton's in a museum display in Tulsa, Oklahoma. Most of it.'

'Well, that's that, I guess. Can't talk to a bunch of bones in a glass case. We sorta figured as much. Anyway,' he said, 'you had something you wanted to tell me?'

'I did. Now I'm wondering what's behind your back.'

'Same as yours, most likely.' Surely he, too, spoke figuratively.

Otherwise, Sander thought, he can see those papers in my pocket. 'Top side and underside of a single story,' said Will. 'Similar to how you told us in a snap where Beau was and didn't even know he existed until a few days ago. So, you wanna start, or should I?'

'How long has it been since any of you have read the Bible?'

There was a long pause. 'We haven't,' said Will. 'Not all of it.'

'Do you believe in God?'

'That question,' Will chuckled, 'always struck me like asking a man on the edge of a cliff if he believes in gravity. It don't matter what he believes, but he can sense he ought to pick his words carefully. We don't have the option to believe or not to believe, Sander. Like your mother, for different reasons, God is as plain to us as that tree you're leaning on. And, like her I would imagine, many of us have thought how nice it would be to make up our own minds, to be able to call it our own decision. Is that what you think you're doing?'

'No. He's there. I realize that. But I have read the Bible, a couple of versions, and I know it pretty well. Well enough, I suppose, to know that a lot of it was originally written about us. Nephilim,' he said.

Will knew the term. Sander carried on. He told of what he had learned from Roger and what he had found on his own, the stuff that made sense and the greater volume of things that confounded him. He talked for almost an hour while his face got blotchy in the cold and his nose ran. He paused to pull the papers from his pocket so he could be sure he was getting this latest part right. He began reading from Psalms 89, interrupting the scripture with Roger's footnotes.

'Please don't do that,' said Will. 'We don't need a Bible lesson.'

'You aint read it. I thought you might like to know what it says.'

'Reading history, if that's what you wanna call it, is not the only way to know things. The person who wrote that had no more clue what really happened than you do. He got the Assembly of the Holy Ones right, but the rest of it sounds like a heap of "O Lord our Heavenly Father gibberish."'

'God's holy council, Roger calls it. He's the pastor at that church I was going to. Gave me this stuff. And further on down here it does mention "the council of the holy ones." Who are they?'

'We weren't exactly sure until a few months ago. We were satisfied with what we had, stories or folklore or just ideas. After you gave us the push, though, we started asking the same question ourselves. There are those of us out there who were alive when God still talked to us. They don't speak English, so it was hard, but we eventually got it worked out.' He stopped. 'It's getting colder. Why don't you build a little fire?'

Sander drew his collar up to his cheeks and blew on his hands. 'I'm fine.'

'These sons of God you mentioned, they make up the Assembly, what your friend calls a council. Same difference. There's untold numbers of them up there and a few were selected to rule at the right hand of God.'

'Sounds like angels.'

'Forget about angels. Think, Congress. God made His heavenly sons long before He made all this stuff.' Sander felt a bump in the ground beneath him, as though Will had tapped a root on the oak. 'And in making everything, He was smart enough, maybe leery enough, to know He could use some help. Like your daddy trusts you around here, so God trusted His heavenly sons. He gave the power of oversight to this Assembly of sons and He listened to their ideas. Together, they set about hashing out rules for everything. Then He started creating.

'People were dandy things. I don't care what your Bible says God thought about em, He and the Assembly all decided they had done good. I mean, just look at em. People are beautiful. Interesting. Unpredictable. And the sons of God who weren't elected to the Assembly, they thought so, too. Especially about the women. In all those rules they had decided on, there wasn't anything at that time to keep God's sons from coming here. It's important you see it that way. No law was broken, because no law about it was on the books. None from the Assembly came, that we know of, but their brothers did.'

Sander wasn't thinking Congress anymore. He had moved on to the British Parliament, then settled on the Roman Senate as the most fitting earthbound analogy.

Will was saying, 'I realize it's crude, and I'm not calling us mules nor saying little people are jackasses. But the sons of God aren't like us. It's a fact – maybe one they didn't consider – that when you go mixing two animals that aren't alike, the stock you end up with can't always carry on breeding on its own. We have enough of our fathers in us to keep having sons, but we evidently can't have daughters. We've always needed people.

'The Assembly took note of this. After the ruckus simmered down and they laid out the law that it could never happen again, they were happy to have sons of their own. Nephilim, they called us, sons who were obliged to live in harmony with people for their own survival. No harm, no foul, they told God. We didn't stand out nearly so much as seventy-ton lizards and we helped God's people. But that aint how God saw it. Assembly or no, He was the Creator.

He made man. Didn't give birth to them as He had done with His sons. He made them with His own hand. And He considered it His sole prerogative to bring beings into creation, or to take them out.'

'So He tried to drown us?' Sander said. 'That aint right.'

'Is that what your friend told you? Cause God did a lot more than that, before and since. Century after century He struck us down wherever His armies found us. All the while the Assembly demanded He stop. They pled for our lives, and they did everything they could to make sure we survived. Like you said, it wasn't right. The Assembly knew we were guilty of nothing. Besides, we were their kids. They talked to us back then and they told us what was going on. Said, "Be patient, God will come around." It was tough for those old guys, I can hear it in their voices, even in foreign languages, and it hurts me.'

'That was the war in heaven?'

'I don't know about any war in heaven, Sander. Sounds like bullshit to me. All I can tell you is what I know from our kin. Things were always very civil, very orderly up there and full of due process. The war was down here. People outnumbered us by the hundreds of thousands. They slaughtered us when they could and otherwise drove us to places where the land was salt and sulfur and nothing would grow. A Nephilim head on a stick was often enough to make a man a king. None of us are sure the little people have forgotten that.'

'They don't hunt us anymore.'

'No. And they wouldn't have God's help if they did. He and the Assembly reached a compromise after a while, like governments always do, and nobody got all they wanted. The upshot is this. Nephilim were cut off. Nobody could speak to us, nobody could help us. That's what God got. In exchange, the Assembly accepted His word that He would have no hand in harming us. And, since we were denied an audience with our creators, we should be able to speak with our forefathers. That's the way it came down. I'm not certain of the date, third or fourth century BC. Nephilim were still attacked sometimes, but that was just man being man. I think God probably counted on that. Could be wrong.'

'It doesn't jive,' said Sander. 'Why is God upset now?'

'I wasn't finished. His sons had thrown the written law in His face. God likely took to studying those laws after that. We're guessing He couldn't find anything that forbade Him fathering sons with women, so that's what He did. We think there were several, Jesus being one. Only, for some reason, God's kids didn't turn out like us. They were seers and prophets and men of magic, but they looked normal. Other little people flocked to these men because they were great teachers. They knew uncommon things because, we believe, they could hear God's voice like we once heard our fathers. At any rate, God had His loophole. Nephilim started dying in greater numbers.'

'The New Testament,' Sander said. His teeth chattered as he shook his head. 'I don't think it mentions us.'

'I would guess not. God found a back door, a way to restore what He thought was right and just. Why would He call attention to it?'

'Restore,' mumbled Sander. 'That's the word Roger used. I kept thinking reconstruct. He said restoration.'

'Do what?'

'Nothing.' Then, 'Did the Assembly ever find out?'

'You're asking if the folks in heaven know about Christianity. I'm gonna go out on a limb and say they do. Our fathers are keeping their end of the bargain. They haven't said a word to any of us since the old deal went down, and we're not seeing too many offspring of God these days, huh? That has us speculating there's some sort of shaky truce up there.'

'Since the time of Christ?' Sander exclaimed. 'How much of this does dad know?'

'Me and your father haven't talked about it. He's grounded in what he does best and has no need for questions like yours. Might be a lesson there. Try keeping your head down, son. Take care of your family first, then yourself, and lastly the ranch. If you've still got time to worry about all this other, get a hobby.'

'That's not good enough.' Sander put both saddle blankets over his shoulder and stood to fold the tarp. 'Oh,' he said. 'I almost forgot. I'm engaged, granddad. Remember the girl I told you about?'

'Alejandra,' said Will.

'Yeah. We'll do it this summer, we think. That was my news. I haven't told mom and dad yet.'

'Her father approves?'

'We're talking about it, how to break it to him. It'll be soon, though.'

'So, you don't have an engagement. You have a proposal. Tell us how that goes, breaking your news to her daddy and all.'

'Are you upset with me now?'

'No, Sander. Just worried, like your dad. Not trying to rain on your parade. Premature congratulations to you and Alejandra. Let us know when you have a date.' As Sander was walking away, Will said, 'And please be careful where you go from here.'

He reached his truck, waited for it to warm up, then drove through the fields toward home knowing that he was just handed an enormous piece of the puzzle Roger had been toiling over the whole of his adult life.

The snow started before he reached the house. Sander walked

in, smelled the boiling cabbage with undertones of salt pork, corned beef hash ready and waiting in covered dishes somewhere, and he realized how long he'd been gone. He took a ladle from the counter and dipped out pot liquor from the peas to warm his throat.

'What'd Will have to say?' asked Jo.

'Told me I needed a hobby.'

'Did you wish Jedediah a happy birthday?'

'It aint his birthday.'

'No, it was last week.'

'Shit.'

'Go in there by the hearth and warm up. Your face is blue,' she told him. 'Lunch will be ready in half an hour.'

Dalton's arms spilled over the sides of the rocking chair and he had his feet propped up near the fire, drying his boots. He was listening.

'I know you don't wanna get back into the art scene, but I hate to see you quit painting. You're good at it. Seems, if you didn't sell them, painting would qualify as a fine hobby. Give us good stuff to hang on the walls, too.'

'Maybe. Except I don't see the benefit in doing something I aint paid for. Do you have a hobby?'

'Yeah,' said Dalton, 'raising a son.'

Sander's comments had little to do with his willingness to return to the studio. Virtually the instant his granddad mentioned a hobby, he was already considering working out his thoughts on canvas. Not to be hung on any walls. Not to ever be seen, but to purge the most troubling images from his mind so, hopefully, he could better cope with the inscrutable mess that was his story. Paper might be the better medium, as it was easier to get rid of. He would pick up some charcoals on his way to Allie's house, if the art supply store was open.

10

Sander was early for dinner at the Sandoval place. It was intentional. From the covered porch, he and Allie could smell the food mingling with the split mesquite Jaime liked to burn in the fireplace. The wind had calmed once the snow began to fall in earnest and they watched the flakes stack higher and higher upon the galvanized top rail of the backyard fence.

'It's time for me to say something, Allie, and I'm not sure how you're gonna take it. Not sure how you *should* take it, is what I mean to say.'

'Stop,' she said. 'It's my fault. I've been scared of papa long enough. I already told my mother that we're getting married sometime this year and she didn't think it would be a big deal. If I start by telling papa that I won't quit school, she says – she hopes – he'll go for it. Doesn't mean he's not going to put you through the ringer, though.'

That was not what Sander had in mind to bring up. Yet it was happy news. She had never given him any assurance she wouldn't talk to her parents about marriage whilst the two of them debated strategy, and he hadn't asked for any. He smiled and took her hand, but thoughts of binding agreements, loopholes, and negotiations in heavenly conference halls left little room in his brain to formulate proper expression of what he felt at that moment. Given time and a stillness of mind, he might have found words. Then again, words were not his forte.

'Today is a good day, then,' he told her. 'After we eat, I'll ask your father for your hand. If he wants me to walk the gauntlet, I've got all evening. Or as long as it takes.'

Allie snickered. 'I don't think it's as serious as all that. He'll ask for details on how you intend to take care of me. Don't take offense. And there's the Catholic thing.'

There's other things too, Sander told himself. There's everything you mean to me that I haven't taken time to say. There's the fact that I've allowed all the rest of this crap to jump ahead of you, to eclipse the single most important thing. He had not taken heed of what his granddad told him about priorities. That would change. He promised himself it would. Evidently not this instant, but soon.

'Got it,' he said. They pressed their cold lips together. Sander pulled away first. 'I wanted to talk to you about meeting my granddad, though.' Thinking on it, he said, 'This isn't easy and it can wait for another time.'

'I know Frank, babe. He's been into the store.'

'He's not the–'

Clarita called from the back door, 'Dinner is ready, Allie.'

He was relieved.

Sander drove up at the ranch shortly before midnight. He came in as quietly as he could, only to find that his mother was waiting for him, working a jigsaw puzzle on the coffee table.

'Is dad asleep?'

'Yeah. He wanted to see how it went over there, but around ten o'clock he said one of you had to be ready for work tomorrow and he went to bed.' She followed his eyes to the stairs, then, 'Well. How did it go?'

'Clarita's tamales are good. Her gravy's kinda watery, but I like salsa with mine anyway.'

'They have enough for you? I've got leftover lasagna if you're hungry.'

'Thanks. I got full.'

'And Jaime?'

'He had enough to eat too, I guess.'

'Sander, I'm tired. Please tell me you talked to him about marrying Allie.'

'How did you–' Sander let it go. She'd always been able to read him at a glance. 'Okay. We talked about it. He aint happy about Allie getting married before she's out of high school, but he understands these are not normal circumstances. He wanted a look at the ranch books to see that we weren't in debt and I told him, all due respect, he could go to hell and wait. But I gave him some round numbers, told him he could call our banker, and suggested he look at his own books. Not once have we asked him for credit. And paid him, I estimate, somewhere in the order of thirty thousand dollars through the second half of last year.'

'He listened to all that?'

'He asked, mamma. Then I told him his grandchild would be raised in his daughter's tradition. I would do everything in my power to make sure the Sandoval heritage was as strong an influence in our kid's life as my own. That aint as hard as he might believe, considering that my heritage is so encumbered by unbelievable nonsense that it's doubtful I'll ever share it with another living soul.'

'You'll rethink that when you have your own boy.'

'Possibly,' said Sander.

'And you've told Allie what to expect along those lines?'

'Yeah, but you and Jaime and Clarita all take it as a given that we want to have a child. There I was agreeing that the kid would be baptized and confirmed a Catholic while I've never seen Allie without her clothes on.' Sander sighed. 'No matter. I don't care who sprinkles water on whom or if somebody in a robe wants to dunk us all in a river.' He stopped to rub his forehead and wobbled a bit when he closed his eyes. 'Rites and rituals notwithstanding, tequila comes from the hind tit of the liquor sow. They ought to strip chassis with that stuff, not drink it. I'm going to bed.'

'You got a date in mind?' she called after him.

'First of June,' Sander said as he mounted the stairs. 'At the courthouse with their padre witnessing. That's the only consideration I wrung out of him all night. See you in the morning.'

Sander heard his dad snoring as he closed his bedroom door.

The calendar seemed to crease and fold inward upon itself over the following week and a half, jumping past whole days and allowing time to slow only when they ran into a frustrating snag in the fields. Sander couldn't recall individual dates to judge whether he had managed the workload to full potential, or whether he had loafed. When he awoke the morning of the tenth and went down the list of things yet undone before the Argos man arrived, he thought he might have stumbled onto what his granddad meant when he talked about the malleability of time. If not, the facts suggested he simply wasn't the foreman for this job. He gave a half-hearted, silent blessing to his crew for the pace of work he was about to saddle them with, and an equally tepid, open prayer of thanks for however many of them came back tomorrow. Sander didn't really know who he was talking to and didn't guess it mattered.

Work commenced at a quarter of six. Men sweated despite the cold and they cursed. They knelt and nursed aches, cuts, and busted thumbnails, then stood up again. At 7.00 PM they fell into their vehicles and drove home. Every one of them came back for more.

By the night of the thirteenth, the place was ready and Sander thought it no small miracle. If anybody looked inside the slaughterhouse, he would discover it to be an empty building. It looked good from the outside, though, and they padlocked the door. No reason for anybody to go in there. For the first night in weeks, Sander slept soundly and did not wake until morning.

Dale Hugh was right on time. He called from the Dallas airport at 6.15 AM and drove up in his rental car two hours later. He greeted Dalton with a business card, Argos Meat Distributors, LLC.

'Good to meet you.' Dalton handed the card to Sander and shook the man's hand. 'My son is the one you wanna talk to.'

Sander shook his hand. Mr Hugh was well over six feet tall and Sander could tell he was used to looking down to speak to people. No doubt he had heard about the Grants, but standing there between them nonetheless took him off guard.

'Is everybody in your family this big?' he asked Sander.

'No. Should we have a look at the facilities first since they're closer?'

The man composed himself. 'If it's all the same to you, I'd prefer to see the stock.'

'Feed lots are in the back,' Sander pointed toward the fields.

'Keeps the smell away from the house. Your car won't make it. You can ride with us if you'd like.'

'How many head are out there?'

'All told, six hundred eighty. Most are breeders. We've set aside a hundred twenty growers and they're just completing their finishing cycle.'

'Where are the breeders?' asked Dale.

'Center pastures, mainly. Bulls in the middle. We'll pass them on the way.'

'Let's walk,' the man said. 'That okay with you?'

'Fine by me,' said Sander, looking down at the polished alligator boots shining below the hem of Dale's jeans. 'It's a far piece, though.'

'I have other boots in the car. If you don't mind, I'll change and we can get started.'

As they walked past, Sander pointed out the semen storage facility, the meat cooler, and the slaughterhouse as though they had been a part of the operation from the start. That's how he wanted it to sound, at least.

'You two run this place by yourselves?' asked Dale.

'It's Sunday,' Sander reminded him.

'Right.'

Dale kept up on the trek to the feed lots. He had a few questions, mainly regarding the age of sires, the condition of the bulling heifers and feed content. Otherwise, they talked little.

When they reached the first feed lot, Dale pushed down the top wire and stepped over the fence without breaking stride. Sander touched his daddy's arm, indicating they should hold back and let the man do his work. There were four dozen animals in the tight space and none were too accustomed to strangers walking among them. Dale moved slowly and deliberately, though. He knew his business and he knew what he was looking for. After twenty minutes, they moved to the next lot. Same story there, but it was a larger space and took the man a bit longer to get close enough to some of the wary calves.

On the walk back, Sander asked, 'Would you like to see our cooler or the semen facility?'

Dale perked up. 'Are you selling the line?'

'No,' said Sander. 'We store semen for our use only.'

'Oh. Thanks, then, but no. Glad to see you've invested in some peace of mind. Far as the cooler goes, if it works, it's fine. Looks a bit on the small side, but then again yours isn't a sizeable operation.'

He left Sander and Dalton to wonder what he meant to accomplish with that remark.

Back at the gate, Dale said, 'I've got some paperwork in the car. Is there somewhere we can sit down?'

'Inside,' Sander said. 'We'll make another pot of coffee.'

At the dinner table, Sander carefully read over the distribution agreement Dale gave him. Twenty-some-odd pages, detailing the rights and responsibilities of each party, and the sliding percentage cut Argos required after all risk was elsewhere assumed or insured against, which percentage ranged from seventeen and a half to thirty. Sander passed the papers to Dalton, who read only the first page. The price per pound offered was twice over what he was used to seeing. He couldn't take his eyes off it.

'Sorry,' said Dale. 'I have another copy of that,' and he reached for his briefcase.

'No need,' said Sander. 'Have you had Grant Beef before?'

'Absolutely. We tested samples from five different domestic outlets.'

'Tested samples,' repeated Sander. 'What I'm asking is, have you personally ever eaten one of our steaks?'

'Yes. Many times.'

'Then,' Sander pointed at the packet Dalton held, 'you know that dog won't hunt. Did you just come out here to see some of the Texas countryside?'

'Mr Grant, I'm very sorry if I've offended you. I meant to do no such thing. It's our standard agreement.'

'And what you inspected out there – those were standard cattle?'

'Sir, we only deal with the best.'

'No,' said Sander, 'I don't think you believe that. Whether you had a Grant sirloin in San Francisco, or one of our ribeyes in Kansas City, you know it was better than anything your company handles.' Dale started to interject, but Sander continued, 'Which means you deal with second-best.'

'Much larger operations–' began Dale.

'We're not talking about the size of the ranch. I gave you our production estimates before you flew your jet down here. What we're talking about is Argos getting Grant Beef at the same price it pays for that other stuff. So I guess we're done talking. There's a few bigger ranches you can visit on the drive back to Dallas. Get your map and I'll show you where they are.'

Dalton's heart was pounding, but he tore his eyes away from the numbers and slid the packet across the table to Dale. Though it pained him, he would do all he could to back his son's play.

Standing, Dalton said, 'I've got to get more feed in those troughs. Nice of you to come out, Mr Hugh.'

The two nodded to one another and Dalton walked out. He forced himself to keep his eyes ahead until he reached the gate. Opening it, he glanced back and saw through the patio door that Sander and Dale remained at the table. He couldn't tell which was talking, or if either one was.

It came time to prepare lunch and Jo couldn't stay out of the kitchen any longer. She walked past the dining table as Sander was putting his pen to some paperwork. She didn't linger, or even speak, but she did notice how many handwritten revisions her boy was initialing. The other man was stoic and didn't seem to see her pass through.

The Grant family celebrated at dinner. Spirits in the house hadn't been so high in years. Never had there been this much con-versation once food was on the table.

'So, what did you say then?' Dalton asked.

'Oh, he wasn't done,' said Sander. 'He had quite a bit to say about how Argos had an obligation to their shareholders and an international supply chain to manage. Keeping in mind, he pointed out, a declining global demand for beef per capita.'

'Really?' asked Jo.

'Really. I wished him luck with that. Hoped they survived the big crisis and all, but said we didn't have any trouble retailing our meat at upwards of seven dollars a pound. Once we were ready to come out with our aged cuts, I said, we could walk all over the price he was offering and do it domestically, without forking over his percentage. And I let him know his percentage was several points higher than his competitors.'

'How did you know he wouldn't leave?'

'I didn't. Not for sure. He came here with Xerox copies of that agreement, prices typed in there no telling when. That pissed me off. Then I noticed the name of our insignificant operation was typed in there as well, before the forms were copied. Before he had even seen the place.'

'Boy, you amaze me sometimes,' said Dalton.

'I just played his game, daddy. His rules. We both knew this ship was about to sail, but he was confused as to who was on the ship and who was dickering from the dock. Once we got that figured out, he made a couple of calls and we came to an agreement. He even offered to leave a little money for the long-distance bill.'

Jo smiled at her husband as she pushed her chair back. 'Eat, yall. I got another pan coming out of the oven.'

The Argos wire transfer arrived in the ranch account a day before the trucks rolled in to load one hundred head. Sander was determined to further increase profit by cutting as much as possible from their processing fees, so within a week of the day Dale Hugh left, he had located and purchased the equipment to finish his slaughterhouse. He had ads in the paper for skilled slaughtermen and packers. Meanwhile, he had every one of his crew working to tool and tweak production – from feed lot to meat cooler. He had another phone line installed in the barn with a big clanging bell ringer he could hear anywhere within sight of the house. It bugged hell out of Jo, but she got used to it.

Both of his parents were happy to see that Sander once again set aside a few hours a week to hole up in his studio. They hadn't realized it, but they missed the smell of his art. He kept the door closed now, which was a change, and he kept his works in progress covered when he wasn't in there. Though they longed to see what he was creating, Jo and Dalton respected his privacy.

In late February, Sander and Allie set a firm date for their nuptials. The ninth of June. The local Justice of the Peace, Howard Ott, collected the fee to preside over the ceremony and open the courthouse annex that Saturday. Their families bemoaned that the couple seemed to approach this occasion more from a logistical vantage than a romantic one. It had helped to bring around Jaime, who revered level-headed decision making despite the fact that emotions often governed his behavior. With the decision made, however, he found himself wanting more for his daughter. Like a traditional Mexican wedding; all the town present to witness the culmination of a fairytale courtship that he had in large part stymied.

Sander and Allie looked at it another way. They enjoyed the most durable romance possible, one that assumed a perpetual bond from their first serious kiss and stood resolute somewhere in their future while they worked out the details. They knew it was an unorthodox way of going about this, but they also knew they couldn't love each other more. Jo thought they were both a little off in the head, and she blamed Sander for most of it.

'That's how you proposed to her?' Jo asked when they told her the story.

'Yeah,' said Sander. 'It worked.'

'Boy, you botched that good.' Then she turned to Allie and said, 'Make him do it again.'

But the couple would not concede that what they shared was anything less than perfect, and Allie sat beside Sander as they informed everyone that the ceremony would reflect their common attitude. They were meant to be together and a grand, theatrical affair would only distract them from that. They would dress up, have the officiating and paperwork done, then move forward as though nothing had changed. Because nothing would change.

'Besides,' Allie told Jo, 'the more you plan, the more things can go wrong. You know?'

'He's brainwashed you, dear,' said Jo.

Clarita agreed, but the two mothers stopped protesting after a while and listened to their kids' idea of a wedding. They wanted vows, prime rib, country music, beer and cake. In that order. If more than ten people showed up, Sander warned, somebody's going home. That included the padre and a photographer.

Though he seriously doubted it would cause Allie to reconsider marrying him, Sander felt, in the interest of full disclosure, he needed to tell her about Will. About all of them buried on the hill by the pond. He decided, however, instead of sitting her down at the house and trying to explain it, he would take her there as his dad had taken him. She wouldn't be able to hear the voices, so it wouldn't be quite as surreal an experience for her, but he expected a degree of shock. He would let Will speak for himself and he would tell Allie what his granddad said, just as she translated for him when her folks lapsed into Spanish. He hoped her disbelief stopped short of her concluding he was delusional.

When they arrived, Will was uncharacteristically reserved. He didn't return the greeting for a few minutes. Sander could hear him breathing, though, and he used this time to tell Allie a little about all the men down there, back to Augustus, with the obvious omission of Bart's brother.

It was not their custom to bring others to this place, but Sander didn't sense Will minded that. Rather, he suspected his granddad's reticence might be simple shyness. He bet none of these men had talked to a woman since they died. Allie's presence likely put them more off balance than she was, since all she heard were the cows in the distance. Other than her fiancé, the only signs of animate life anywhere nearby were the circling shadows from a pair of turkey vultures riding a thermal overhead. She listened to Sander, though, as he passed along Will's polite salutation.

Then Sander decided better of soft-pedaling the message and told her, 'Actually, what he said was, "Nice job, kid. Have her thinking you're nuts before she even moves in." *Then* it was, "Good afternoon, Alejandra."'

'Is this your way of telling me we're gonna live with your parents?' She gave him no time to respond. 'The ranch is your life, babe. Our life, soon. I always expected to live here. Can we think about building our own little place, separate from the big house, though?'

Sander's ear was tuned to Will's voice.

Allie giggled. 'Has he got something else to spring on me?'

'No,' said Sander, after a moment. 'He wishes us every happiness. And I'll build you whatever kind of place you want. Let's go back to the house.'

That would have to be the end of it, for now. Anything Sander might offer to convince her, Will reminded him, would necessarily involve a history lesson. Which, in her case, likely meant documentation of some sort. Was he prepared to go there again?

It was obvious the ninth of June was going to be a beautiful day even before the first orange hint of the sun. Sander's only lingering worry was the ring he had special ordered, whether it would arrive in time and whether it would be as impressive as he imagined. It came in on Thursday and exceeded his greatest hopes. Allie would love it. Whereas, Sander loved being able to give her something so extravagant. Going on twelve years old, he was master of a business enterprise that would make them rich before his eighteenth birthday, carry the Grant name to distant countries, and provide a life for them none of his ancestors dared wish.

After replacing, at Dalton's insistence, the portion of his personal savings he had used to finance recent improvements, Sander was well-heeled on all fronts. Aside from a touch of cold feet, which Jo had warned him about, he felt there could be no finer hour to take his bride. Early on his wedding day, having eaten all the breakfast his nervous stomach would tolerate, he retreated to his studio. No longer a place to toil at his craft, the room was his safe harbor now, whatever storms may come. He laid on canvas and paper those burdens too cumbersome to carry and always left with a brighter outlook and a renewed confidence about the future. He often didn't know what would come out of him when he sat down at his easel. His hands did, though.

Evidently, the heaviest thing on his mind this morning was his father, so that's what his fingers set out to paint. With his palette knife he mixed a deep walnut brown for Dalton's hair, and he added more and more Titanium White until it seemed right. When he was satisfied with the color, before making the first stroke, he stared at it and realized what he had done. The smear of paint was dusty gray, the brown in it barely noticeable. Instead of starting with an inch of white and adding just a dab of Translucent Brown, Sander had begun with a ten-year-old memory of his dad and he'd used nearly a whole tube of paint lightening his hair to the color it now was. He dropped the dry brush back into the jar with the others, wiped his palette clean with a paper towel and went to shave and shower. His tuxedo might need a last minute touch-up on the hems, he thought.

Frank didn't get drunk until late in the afternoon, back at the ranch. When he reached his tipping point, Jaime wasn't far behind. They all fit around two tables placed end to end in the yard, sweating in their formal clothes and not minding it much, commenting as they wiped their brows that it was better, there being no wind.

Laughter spread down one side of the chairs and returned on the other. If the thing could've gone better, none present could imagine how. It was, thought Jo, the best omen for a strong union. At their kids' request, nobody spent much on gifts. Instead, they shared equally in the work of pulling off the event, and the cleaning up afterward. In between, they enjoyed one another. Sander and Allie, thought Clarita, were too young to know how rare a thing this was. A flawless thing.

The only snag regarding the date, Sander had warned Allie, was that it fell on the start of weaning season. There wouldn't be time for a honeymoon. She didn't care. They could take one later, or not at all.

As their parents and Frank and Doris started taking in the dishes from the banquet tables, Sander desired some time alone with his wife. He didn't have anything special to say. They had said it all. He just wanted to look at her when nobody else was looking. He allowed that selfishness wasn't only acceptable in this case, but a big part of why he married this lady, Alejandra Grant.

Allie kicked off her heels in the grass, gathered the modest train of her dress, and walked with Sander to the far side of the barn. He leaned back against the plank wall and pulled her close.

'I've made space for you in my bedroom,' he said.

'I didn't even bring my stuff, baby. I thought we could move it all once things slowed down for you.'

'You don't need your stuff. Not tonight. My bedroom aint much, but I'm gonna make you a spot in my studio, too. I want you to design us a house.'

'I can't draw.'

He tapped her head. 'If it's in there, we'll get it out. I'll help you,' he said. 'Spend the night with me?'

Dalton had watched them disappear around the corner and he thought about Jo when she was eighteen. His son was so fortunate to begin this part of his life now. He was as happy as a father could be, and more tired than he thought a man could survive. Once Sander and Allie were out of sight, he kissed his wife on her neck and told her he would load up the tables and chairs in the morning to take them back to the rental place. He needed out of his suit and he needed a shower, if he had the energy. Jaime and Frank bid him goodnight. The other women wanted to hug his neck, then he was thankfully inside and loosening his necktie. The doorbell rang.

Dalton found Jason on the doorstep, bearing a gift. Looked about the size of a cutlery set. He might've guessed the brash young man would do something like this. He was Sander's problem, though. Or Jo's.

'I just ... I,' stuttered Jason, 'wanted to wish the newlyweds well. Have I come at a bad time?'

'They're all still out there,' said Dalton, throwing a thumb over his shoulder. 'I'm done for the day.'

Jason thanked Dalton and offered an awkward congratulations to him, too, as the big man lumbered up the steps. He couldn't see the bride and groom out the patio door. The folks out there looked to him like they were wrapping things up. There was more light from the porch now than from the setting sun. He put his gift and a card from his pocket on the dining table and thought he would leave them be. Maybe visit another day. On his way past the stairs again, curiosity snared him with a grip he hadn't felt since he broke the stranglehold of amphetamines.

Jason heard the shower kick on up there and took one more glance out back. Nobody would be the wiser if he had a quick peep in Sander's studio. No artist, he thought, drops his brushes cold turkey. As Sander's mentor, surely he had some minuscule remnant of privilege here. At least to see, he reasoned, what his protégé was creating.

11

Jo helped Allie move her things on Sunday, after the Sandovals returned from church. She didn't have much that she wanted to take with her, preferring to leave behind what she considered childish things. Jo urged her to take enough of her personal items, precious belongings, to make her new space feel like home.

'There's plenty of room,' she told Allie, 'and Sander would want you to.'

Clarita said she would pack the rest and save it for her daughter, in case she wanted anything else.

Meanwhile, Sander set about organizing his studio. It was in way of a surprise for Allie. He would more than make a spot for her in here. He would make her an equal.

First, there was something he needed to do. He lined the wall with his recent charcoals, propping them up in what he estimated was the order he'd done them. With one more look, he sought some durable guarantee of the purpose served in their creation. Reasons, in the abstract, for the symbols drawn in this little room might get him closer to a fundamental reason, might they not?

One way or the other, he felt he must understand something here, and it wasn't coming readily.

He recalled finishing some of the pieces, but the style was un-recognizable. He had to wonder from whence these images came. Before him was a chronicle of the sordid business between God and giant, stripped to monochrome detail. In places, the black was pressed hard into the paper, layer on layer, until it sweated charcoal, a liquid absence of light that glistened.

They began with the coupling, an angelic figure entangled with the curves of a woman, all reflected in the white of a great eye looking elsewhere. Next was the birth of the half-heavenly, an oversized infant spreading the pelvis of a woman, tearing skin with a veined arm. A divine covey stood watch in this one, ignoring the grotesque agony. The council scene followed; robed and statuesque men defiant in the face of God. Ape teeth bared, tendons of the neck taut like bowstrings, and all mouths were open at once in argument. Then giants were dying. Three separate pieces showed cyclopean bodies in various states of demise, their anatomies spilled over the lines of an earth-like palm or at the tip of an impossible finger. The birth of Jesus was later in the sequence, somehow depicted with spite. And the rest narrated a struggle with no triumph. Death, contention, and compromise were merely a backdrop. The intended feel seemed that of an endless tragedy from the seed of a feckless act. On those terms, the chronicle was an undeniable success. The cause so clearly inadequate to provoke such effect that the whole thing made just as much sense in reverse.

Individually, these pictures weren't just ugly. They were divested of beauty to an extent as to be aesthetically perfect. The best work he had ever done. And they originated in a place that had no name, no trail leading back. Sander was forced to conclude that an abyss could fall upon a person, or sidle beneath him. It was a sobering thought, that such darkness without bottom could visit him like a posthypnotic suggestion, when and where it chose. It could speak through his practiced hand, then vanish, immune to all thereafter. Then that was the purpose, he decided. Because despair was in the dread of such a trespassing void. Giving over to it renders everything meaningless. Reasons. Depression. The void itself.

As irony would have it, Sander's morbid epiphany was what enabled him to put the work away, marveling at how he had found the time to do all this drawing. He stacked them, wrapped them in craft paper and crisscrossed the bundle with row after row of tape. For now, he slid it onto the highest shelf in the closet, thinking he would probably put it out with the garbage next time he saw it, or the time after that, or whenever he no longer lusted for control over that kind of talent. He began filling the space around it with everything in the room he didn't need at the moment.

When he was done, the closet was packed floor to ceiling. He had to put his shoulder into the door to latch it. For the sake of time, and because he didn't give a shit, he applied no effort whatever to ordering or cataloging the contents. The stuff was out of the way. A few old boxes remained in one corner of the room. Likely garbage as well, but they presently served as shelf space for the few art supplies not stuffed in the closet. Other than that, there was his easel and chair, and the normal-sized ones Jason had used which Sander would bequeath to Allie. He erased both the chalk boards whereon he scrawled random notes to himself, and he scoured the walls of all the paper scraps, photos, and bold quotations he'd pinned there over the years. The studio was ready.

Allie was overjoyed at the trouble he had gone to, and she told him so. But she stared at her empty easel there beside his for a bit too long. Jo stood in the doorway with one of Allie's suitcases.

'What?' Sander asked.

'I'm telling you I can't draw,' said Allie. 'Not even a little bit. Stick figures and smiley faces, maybe. Right next to the famous Sander Grant.'

'Don't be nervous,' he said. 'What you need is a big flip pad to start with. Cheap paper and a number two pencil.'

'Thanks for the vote of confidence.'

'No, listen. It'll help you get started. Pencil lines can be erased and paper can be thrown away. Whenever you want, just give me the word and I'll get you any medium you need. Canvas, clay, limestone.'

She laughed then nodded. 'Okay.'

Allie looked up at Sander for a second, then jumped to kiss him on the cheek, making it only to the middle of his arm. Jo had seen her do this a few other times. How long would it be until her boy learned to feel when his wife wanted to kiss him, and began to bend down for her like Dalton did? She could say something to Sander about it, but she remembered sorting out the little things like that on their own when she first moved out here. She recalled talking with Dalton those first few months, giggling, figuring stuff out. It was part of the wonder of these men, that they didn't seem to realize their loved ones existed, physically, on a lower plane. Jo decided against reducing it to a lesson on giant etiquette.

'Mom,' said Sander, 'most of my closet is cleared out and half of the drawers. If there aint enough room, box up some more of my stuff and I'll go through it later. All I need to get to is my boots and work clothes.'

'We'll take care of it,' she told him. 'Go help your dad.' When she saw the wrapped box from Jason and the unopened card on Sander's dresser, she called, 'Why didn't you open this gift?'

'Because I'm mailing it back to him. Put it wherever,' Sander hollered on his way downstairs. He went to look for Dalton and found him in the east pasture, bent and checking the back legs on a heifer.

'What's up?' he said, startling his dad.

'To tell the truth, I don't know. This one and a few others just seemed a little jumpy when I got close.' He turned loose the animal and it wobbled, almost imperceptibly, then kicked at the air a couple of times with its back leg, like it had mud stuck in its hoof. 'Aint nothing wrong with her hooves.'

'Strange,' said Sander. 'You think the heat got to em?'

'I can't figure. It aint that hot out here.' Dalton dusted off his hands. 'Seth's coming tomorrow to have a look at a few of the smaller calves we're about to take off the teat. Let's see what he says.'

For the remainder of the afternoon, they drove the pastures together and corralled every animal that looked 'kinda off', as they took to calling it. There were eight, all of them female, and the men put them together in a holding pen.

Seth Craig, the senior vet at Dixon Animal Hospital and treating physician for Grant cattle, showed up promptly at 8 AM. Though Dr Craig was now in his early sixties, he hadn't moved to Dixon until shortly before Will died and so wasn't one of the vets Dalton was used to seeing when he was a kid. Soon after he arrived in town, however, the other vets at the Animal Hospital began qualifying their commentary and delaying their treatment of Grant cattle pending a consultation with this fella Seth Craig. Dalton decided to cut out the middle man and told the others to just send Dr Craig.

The first time Dalton actually met him – short, potbellied, balding, and incredibly brash in tendering his judgment on everything from the proper way to make iced tea to the benefits of square-baled hay – he wondered was this strange diminutive character the best choice to care for Grant cattle. He didn't have to wonder long. Not only was Craig better educated in his field than any doctor Dalton had run across, but he had an intuition of his own that sometimes rivaled Dalton's.

The three men shook hands at the yard gate. Seth was eating a pastry and he shoved the last third of it in his mouth and wiped bits of icing from his gray handlebar mustache.

He threw a thumb over his shoulder and said, 'Got this intern with me from UT. That okay with you?'

Dalton looked back and saw a girl with a blonde ponytail in the doctor's truck. 'Yeah,' he said.

'How's the wife?' he asked Dalton.

'She's doing fine. Sander got married on Saturday.'

'So they tell me. Congratulations,' he said without evident conviction. It was his way, his customary deadpan delivery, and it took some getting used to. 'Here's a tip,' he told Sander. 'Hug her more often. I didn't realize that hugs don't cost me nothing until Cheryl died last year.'

'I hadn't heard, Seth. I'm sorry.'

'Yeah, it's been a real bitch, but what are you gonna do? Keep moving. Oh, and thanks for the invite to the damned wedding. Had you a shiny new toaster and everything.'

Before they got in their trucks to drive over to the holding pen, Dr Craig asked Dalton what he thought was wrong with the stock he and Sander had separated.

'I tell ya, it's not like something you would really notice at a glance. If they were men, I'd say they were hungover. They might be fine today.'

'I'd say, if you thought that was likely, you wouldn't have penned em up,' Seth retorted.

Dalton was worried and Sander could see it as well as Seth. He rode with his dad and they listened to the suspension of the old ranch truck creak and ping across the field. Privately, he believed Dalton might be suffering from exhaustion and Sander wished he had been the one to discover the wobbly stock, instead of farting around in the studio this morning.

When they arrived at the pen, Sander closed the east gate behind both trucks then joined his dad and Seth. It was possible two of the heifers were ten pounds lighter than the others. It was possible they weren't. None were kicking the air or otherwise behaving oddly. Even Dalton took a minute to figure out which ones he wanted examined first. Once he did, Sander grabbed two short lengths of rope from behind the truck seat, hopped the pen rail and quickly heeled the ones Dalton pointed out. The first one stopped lowing and struggling against the rope when Sander put his knee on her neck.

Off the cuff, Seth said he couldn't see that anything was wrong with either of them. Dalton told him that they seemed better today, but he pointed out how they had been standing apart from the others, how they looked – what? – nervous. They looked nervous, he thought. Seth wasn't buying it. Normal temperature, normal appearance, clear eyes, good reflexes, no visible wounds.

'They didn't seem too nervous when your boy flopped em,' he said.

'They were, though. Yesterday they were fidgety, aloof. I can't explain it.'

'Aloof? There's a five-dollar word.'

'Or something,' Dalton added, looking back at their trucks. 'Does she ever get out?'

'Rachel? Sometimes. I told her yall don't like strangers around your cattle. She's a timid soul.' He rose and put his hands on his hips, shaking his head at the prone animal.

'What do you think?' Dalton asked.

'I'll put them through the paces,' he said, 'as many tests as you want me to run. But humans don't have the market cornered on antisocial behavior, you know.'

'Please,' said Dalton. 'It would have me sleeping better.'

'Is that what's wrong with you? You're the one looks like you might need some tests,' the doctor said. 'If you don't mind me saying.'

Sander said, 'Give them all the full workup, doc. We'll be at the chutes.'

'I'll need Rachel's help,' he said.

'Is she up to it?' asked Sander.

'I hope so. She's kinda pretty. Be a shame if she got trampled.'

They left Seth and Rachel to it. Sander closed the gate again behind his dad's truck, climbed back in and said, 'He's a weird little man.'

'The best vet in three states. Don't doubt it.'

'I have to say, I can't see anything wrong with those cows today.'

'Experience is good for something, son.'

'You feeling alright?'

'Yeah. Why?'

'You do look a little pale this morning.'

'I'm not awake, I guess.'

'You didn't eat much breakfast. Why don't you let mamma cook you something else?'

'Yeah. I'll do that.'

This further worried Sander. He was ready for his dad to blow off the suggestion, or even tell him to mind his own business. He expected it. He had never seen Dalton leave the fields during the day unless there was pressing business inside.

'Drive on up to the house and I'll walk back down,' said Sander.

'No need. The walk will do me good.' Dalton didn't want Sander up at the house making a big deal out of a little fatigue, getting Jo worried. He pulled up beside the chutes and cut the engine. 'I won't be long,' he said.

Sander watched him start across the field. Maybe he was right. Maybe he was only groggy this morning. With all that had been going on, he couldn't imagine any of them were as rested as they could be.

Once his dad was well out of earshot, he said, 'Take it easy on yourself.' Then he joined the Smitherman brothers and went to work.

From the chutes to the house was only a quarter of a mile. Dalton walked briskly for the first minute. He knew his son was watching him. Then he glanced back and saw Sander busy with the guys and he stopped to catch his breath. A quarter mile never seemed so far. He wanted to stretch out in the grass. When his breathing slowed, he started walking again, much slower. His legs were piles driven deep into the soil with each step and his shoulders began to sway with the effort of wrenching them free. He blinked sweat from his eyes. Then he fell.

Lying with one arm beneath his belly, the side of his face pressed into alfalfa stubble, he took in the scents of his land. The first day of October would be upon them again in less than four months. Another weaning season come and gone, the herd building itself for next year's market, and the clumps of purple three-awn would be sending up their lacy flags in patches. Mixed with the reddish plumes of switch grass and dotted with bluebonnets, the pastures would be an undulating tapestry beneath fall-gray skies, stretching to the far tree line. Their bouquet would soon ride upon the pollen, borne by the north autumn wind across the backs of the herd, lifting their musk before filtering in through the window screens. Jo would keep the windows open for him, even though the ragweed from the fallow pastures made her sneeze. The dandelion wine she set aside last July would ease her hay fever in the evenings and add to the season its own special sweetness, with the ginger and citrus from her breath. He would be here to see his son enjoy that with his new wife.

He pushed himself up and turned to check that Sander wasn't barreling across the field to scoop him up and carry him home. Nobody had seen him fall. He maintained his momentum this time, all the way to the patio door.

After getting Allie off to school that morning, Jo had decided to catch up on some reading. She was on the couch when she heard the door open.

She walked into the dining room and asked, 'Is he done already?'

'Who?' said Dalton.

'The vet.' She walked up close to his broad chest and tugged on the front of his shirt. 'Honey, you've got grass in your hair.' He leaned down and she picked it out. His thick head of hair had become eiderdown. She smoothed it. 'Why don't you take a little nap?'

'I'm hungry. Seth will stop by the house when he's done and I want to talk to him.'

'Sit down. I'll make you some eggs. I knew you didn't eat enough.'

'Meat,' he said.

'You want sausage?'

He fell into his chair with a sigh and squeezed his temples with one hand. 'Headache for some reason.' Then, 'My meat. A steak.'

'I think everything's frozen except a sirloin and a chuck roast.'

'That's fine.'

'Which?'

'Both.'

She asked him what he wanted with it and he said water. She seared the steak in a skillet and started him with that, then cut the roast in pieces, floured and pan-fried them like stew meat. She asked him again if he could wait for her to put together a proper meal. No, he could not. He ate it all, very slowly, and she didn't know what to say to him. She was rubbing his shoulders, kissing the top of his head, smelling of him the way he smelled the land.

Dr Craig knocked on the patio door and slid it open.

'Jo.'

'Seth.'

'Something smells good. What's cooking?' he asked her.

'What would you like?'

'Some of those flapjacks with fruit on em like they do down at IHOP.'

'I'll see what I can do,' she said.

'Naw. Forget it. I'll stop by over there on my way back. I just thought you might have some lying around.'

'Coffee?'

'That stuff will kill you,' he said, and took a seat beside Dalton.

'I'll leave you two, then.'

When she was gone, Seth said, 'No kidding, big fella. You look like hell.'

'What's wrong with my cattle?'

'How should I know? Probably nothing. Rachel and I took blood and stool samples. I'll call you when I'm finished with the labs. All your calves look fine to come off the milk.'

'Did you tell Sander?'

'No. I don't work for Sander.'

'Yes you do. He's foreman now.'

'Tell him yourself. And get some sleep. Doctor's orders.'

Three hours later, Sander came in for lunch and was pleased when Jo told him his dad was sleeping. That portion of his plan as foreman which, for the blasphemy of it, he hadn't mentioned to anyone and refused to think too loudly about, would come out over dinner. A subsistence ranch, or one in the struggling stages of profitability, was a self-imposed sentence of hard labor with no waking reprieve. No longer was that the case for Grant Beef. He and Dalton both would be putting in less hours, supervising more and taking less in hand. Especially his dad. They employed ten men now, all of them capable and experienced but, since the construction was done, they were underworked. They should earn their wages, and from this point on, they would.

Sander knew there would be some grumbling, maybe a minor argument over this, but he hoped the first of their disagreements Allie witnessed wouldn't draw out into a week-long drama.

After lunch, his dad worked at a steady pace until six o'clock. His spirits seemed better and the nap had taken care of his pallor. They walked to the house together and the women were waiting on them in the kitchen.

Sander bellied up to the table and studied his reflection in a butter knife. While Jo and Allie placed the food between them, he announced, 'I think that's the last twelve-hour workday we'll spend in the pasture, you and me.' He looked across at his dad.

To his surprise, Dalton didn't object, saying only, 'It's about time you let up on us.'

Well. There it was, then. Sander didn't feel like pushing his luck and clarifying that he had no intention of letting up on the hired help. Nor did he think it wise to qualify his proclamation where it pertained to him alone. He didn't personally rule out throwing in a long day with the field hands when the need arose. And he knew it would.

Seth Craig drove out again five days later, unannounced. Sander heard the truck and noticed the doctor had a younger fellow with him: a skinny man, long-faced with wire-rim spectacles. Another university intern, he suspected. It was coming on late afternoon and Sander was trying to find a stopping point outside so he could get to some paperwork. The two men climbed from the doctor's truck and Sander met them at the gate. The skinny one fixed on him as though he were an approaching tornado.

'Sander, this is Eliot Drew. Or Drew Eliot, I'm not sure. He's come to have a look at those heifers. Render his expert opinion, if that's okay.'

Sander shook his hand. The man stared up blankly, mouth slightly open.

'He aint thick,' Seth said. 'He's English. Pretty good vet from what I gather.'

'Dr Drew Eliot. It's a pleasure.' Now, the best he could do was keep his gaze moving, roving the ground and the land behind Sander like he had some affliction.

'You get the results from those tests?' Sander asked Seth.

'Everything's normal.'

'I don't understand.'

'Goddamn busybodies,' Seth said. 'I was chatting it up with some idiot in Oklahoma, about your heifers, and he told somebody who told somebody else because neither of us had any good ideas. Next thing I know, here comes Drew.'

'Mr Grant, I'm a veterinary pathologist, working with your Department of Agriculture.' He handed Sander a card with USDA on it. 'We've seen abnormalities like those you reported. It's possible I can help Dr Craig in this. Have you quarantined the animals?'

'Quarantined?'

'Have you put them in a separate area, away from the other stock?'

'I know what it means. We moved the corral pen behind the barn where we could keep an eye on em.' He looked to Seth and Seth shrugged. 'I checked this morning. They were fine.'

The three of them rounded the corner of the barn and Seth stopped in his tracks. One animal appeared fine. It stood absolutely still, staring through the fence in the far corner of the pen and didn't turn at the sound of the men. The other ones, however, they looked, like Dalton had said, badly hungover or even drunk. They would weave a few steps, then their front legs would buckle. Each time, the heifers caught their balance before they fell, but they looked far from okay. Their heads lolled and looked too unwieldy for them to support much longer. Sander stopped behind Seth and Dr Eliot kept walking to the fence.

'What is it?' Sander asked. 'What's wrong with em?'

'I'm not sure,' Seth admitted.

The Brit leaned on the fence and watched the animals with no visible reaction. Then he turned to Seth, 'You've checked for bites?'

'A week ago.'

'Full blood chemistry?'

'Yes,' Seth said.

'Lead poisoning?'

'There are no toxic levels of lead or anything else.'

Dr Eliot turned to Sander, 'How old are these animals?'

'Three to four years, on average.'

'Do you have them on supplements?' Eliot asked.

'Yes.'

'May I see what you use?'

Seth nodded to Sander. It was more than a little troubling seeing Seth out of his depth, deferring to this foreigner. Sander led them into the barn, where Dr Eliot stood looking at the feed sack labels. It was a three-brand proprietary recipe Sander had settled on, the pallets were arranged in aisles for easy tractor loading. The Brit tore away the plastic wrap from one pallet and took a close look at the label beneath.

'Yes,' he said. 'I recognize this one. Is all your stock on this particular supplement?'

'Yeah. Rotated on it, at least,' Sander said. 'The yearlings have been on it since weaning. Why?'

'In 1986 we diagnosed a brain disease among British cattle. Bovine Spongiform Encephalopathy.'

'Mad Cow,' said Seth.

'And?'

'And your heifers out there seem to have it,' Dr Eliot told him.

'Seem to?' Then, to Seth, 'You said the tests were normal.'

Dr Eliot answered, 'There is no BSE test for living animals. It requires examination of brain tissue.'

'You have to put them down to see what's wrong with them?'

'They'll be dead in a week, Mr Grant.'

'If that's what they've got,' Seth added.

'It is,' said Dr Eliot. 'Were it one animal, I would leave open the possibilities of meningitis and listeriosis. But not in so many heifers of the same age, otherwise healthy, and on this supplement. To a near certainty, it is BSE.'

Sander asked, 'Is it contagious?'

'Our best guess is it's contracted only through feed supplements containing prions from infected animals.'

'Cattle remains in the food,' said Seth.

Which prompted Sander to ask, 'You knew about this?'

'I knew of the possibility, yes. Late yesterday. There hasn't been a recorded case in Texas.'

'What do we do?' asked Sander.

'For the stock? Nothing,' Dr Eliot told him. 'It's invariably fatal and there is no treatment. Have you sold any three-year-old cattle this year?'

'Not yet.'

'Any culls?'

'Not yet,' Sander said again. Then he asked, 'How do we find out which ones are sick?'

'You don't. Not until they're symptomatic.'

'Well, you're full of answers.' He turned to Seth. 'One more time. Why did you bring him here?'

'I wanted to rule it out. That's all. I was sure it was something else. I'm sorry, Sander.'

Dr Eliot answered for himself, 'I'm part of a USDA surveillance program. Until further notice, you cannot sell any cattle from this herd. I'll report my findings to the Department and they will contact you shortly. Meanwhile, I have some suggestions for you and your family. We aren't sure whether, or how, Creutzfeldt-Jakob Disease among humans is related to BSE.' Sander was walking toward the house and heard Dr Eliot warn him to dispose of any beef in the freezers.

Inside, Jo said, 'Is that Dr Craig's truck?'

'Yeah.'

'Who's that with him?'

'Some English guy. Where's dad?'

'Taking up some grass in the front yard so I can have an herb garden. Allie went to the grocery store for me.'

Sander walked out the front door. He heard Dalton grunting on the side of the house opposite the driveway. He walked around and saw the sod was cut from the base of a pin oak. The tree was about ten inches in diameter, one they had been talking about trimming back because the branches scraped paint off the eaves when a hard wind blew. It now leaned away from the house at a forty-five degree angle. Dalton's head was down, both arms straightened against the trunk, pushing the tree. With each shove, the tree swayed and groaned.

'What're you doing?'

'Your mamma wanted to keep this if we could,' Dalton panted. 'But I dug down and saw its roots are heaving the foundation.' He took a rag from his back pocket and wiped his forehead. 'It's got to go.'

'Did you cut the roots going under the house?'

'Yeah. Let me take care of this. What's up?'

'We need to talk. Seth was just here.'

'Let's go inside,' said Dalton. 'I need a drink. It's hot today, huh?'

'I guess.' Sander let his dad walk past. 'Give me a minute to get the guys working on something else. I'll be right in.'

When Dalton disappeared around the corner of the house, Sander looked up to the top of the tree. It was about thirty feet tall, a healthy canopy, and he hated to see it leaning. He looked at the hole his dad had been straddling. The roots were severed on the house side. The axe lay in the grass beside a shovel. He circled the oak and rubbed his palm on the bark, cold to the touch and moist. He felt sorry for the tree. Or something. He felt deeply sorry for something.

He crouched under the trunk on the leaning side, braced it on his shoulder and stood up. A rapid series of pops and great clods of red dirt came out of the hole. Sander walked a few yards with it, then dropped the tree to the ground and went inside.

Dalton said, 'Your mom told me Seth had an Englishman with him.'

'Yeah.'

'Fee! Fie! Foe–' That's all Dalton could get out before he looked at Jo and started laughing again.

Sander was glad to see him in such a good mood. He hated to spoil it, but waiting with this news wouldn't help matters. 'We've got a problem with the herd.'

'What is it?'

'Something called BSE. It's a brain disease. Seth thinks those heifers have it. The fella who came with him is some sort of expert. He's working for the USDA.'

'The Englishman?'

'Yeah, dad.' He let go a barely perceptible smile. 'The Englishman.'

'Well, you've got to be able to handle this sort of thing.' He pulled Jo to him with both arms. 'I have herb gardens to plant!'

'It's serious.'

'Trust Seth,' Dalton told him. 'Whatever he says we need to do. Vaccinations or what?'

'No. There's no treatment.'

'So we're gonna lose the heifers?'

'All but one are nearly dead already. The um ... This fella says the USDA will be in touch.' Sander shook his head. 'The whole herd is quarantined.'

'Do what?'

'It's the feed. The protein supplement, there's evidently something in the supplements I ordered from over there.'

'It gave this disease to the whole damned herd?'

'I don't know. They don't know for sure. It's just what he said.'

Jo sat with them and Sander told everything he'd gleaned from Seth and Dr Eliot, but there wasn't much more to say. When he got to the part about the meat in the freezer, Jo spoke up.

'There's nothing wrong with that meat. Did you tell him we've been eating it and there's nothing wrong with us? There's nothing wrong with that meat.'

'I didn't, mamma. I'm assuming the people from the Department will tell us what to do next.'

'And we can't sell any until they do,' Dalton said. Then he asked, 'Are there any others showing symptoms of this thing?'

'Not that I saw.'

'How much will it cost to test the whole herd?'

'There's no test. That's what Dr Eliot says. I figure there has to be. I want to talk to the USDA people and find out what they know.'

Jo came to bed sometime after midnight. Dalton stared at the ceiling.

'What did God say?' he asked her.

'Nothing. Either He wasn't listening or I made Him mad. I sort of blamed Him. Still do.'

'Is that wise?'

'It's Him or my boy.'

Sander and Allie had retired to their bedroom after dinner. She had more questions than he had information about this thing. He patiently repeated 'I don't know' until she'd exhausted nearly all avenues.

She asked, 'Is it my papa's fault?'

'Partly.'

'Is it your fault?'

'Yes.'

Jo and Allie were on eggshells the following morning. Neither knew what to say to her man. They weren't even talking much to each other. Jack Loren from the USDA showed up as they finished breakfast. He brought another man along who evidently spoke for the higher-ups at the Food and Drug Administration, but had no business card.

Allie invited the men in and sat them at the dinner table. They said they'd each have a coffee, but no food. Sander excused himself briefly to dismiss the hands who'd shown up for work and were mumbling in a tight circle at the yard gate. He asked Javier to stick around until the last hand arrived for the morning and tell him he had the day off as well.

Back inside, the FDA man was passing out brochures on Creutzfeldt-Jakob Disease, called CJD, even though this guy insisted on pronouncing it 'Yay-kub.' It was, he said, the human version of what was happening to the cattle, transmissible through BSE infected beef. The text was stupefying in its naked horror. Insomnia, personality changes, blindness, dementia, memory failure, involuntary muscle jerks, and coma. The progression marched onward like time itself and there was no cure. Everyone died. This was meant, Sander concluded, to scare his mom into disposing of three freezers of meat. It had another purpose in Loren's orderly presentation, to be revealed momentarily.

Jack Loren said, 'We will need those infected heifers for autopsy.' Then he asked Dalton, 'Do you have livestock insurance for the rest of the herd?'

Dalton looked to Sander, who nodded. Thus, Mr Loren began addressing Sander. 'They won't pay for disposal. I know. I used to be an underwriter. It's alright, though. The Department will conduct that operation in the name of public health. The USDA will pay you fair market value for the beef by weight, but nothing for breeding stock value or loss of profit. That's where your insurance should kick in.'

Jo said, 'Wait a minute. You can't waltz in here and tell us, just tell us that we have to ... You can't just destroy the whole herd.'

'Yes ma'am, we can. But you don't want to do it like that, under government order. I'll tell you why. If you're properly insured, you'll recover your investment in the herd sires and brood cows. Dr Craig says you've stored semen and we have no reason to believe it presents any threat. We'll expunge the BSE from your land, destroy the culprit feed, and there'll never be a USDA ban or recall on Grant Beef. From the timeline your son provided to Dr Eliot, it seems you haven't sold any potentially contaminated meat so far this year – that would be cattle over the age of thirty months.' He turned to Sander, 'Have you?'

'No.'

'Good. The disease normally doesn't show itself or, as far as we know, become transmissible until after three years of age. That's probably why you have so few symptomatic cattle. After we dispose of the present stock, hopefully you can start again.'

'How do you know there's any more sick ones, then?' Jo demanded.

Mr Loren thought out his response before speaking. When he did, he addressed everyone, Allie included, and he decided to go back to his point regarding the future, instead of arguing scientific jargon with them. He was well trained.

'Doing it my way, voluntary destruction of the herd, keeps this out of the papers. The Grant name is untarnished and you build back up. If we come with an order, it's public record. News stations will run clips from England, cattle stumbling around just like your sick heifers. And this information?' He held up one of the CJD brochures. 'This will be in every grocery store. Nobody will care that this herd is destroyed and the feed supplement isn't used anymore. They'll never buy Grant Beef again. Every ranch in Texas will be cut to the bone. The nationwide beef market will suffer.'

'We watched it happen in Britain,' said the other man. 'They couldn't give away their meat for free.'

'We get it,' Dalton said.

Allie squeezed Sander's hand.

'Look,' Loren said, 'I've come to help in every way I can. We don't want our beef suppliers going out of business. We can leave you with a presumptive diagnosis today, in writing. Get it to your insurance company. They're going to tell you that governmental action isn't covered by your policy. Give them my card as well. Tell them it's not a governmental action. The herd will be put down for humanitarian purposes. I'll support you on that. If they won't go for it, our Risk Management Agency will explain to your company, in detail, how little help they'll get in future crop claims if they don't step up to bat here. We have strings to pull.'

'Get rid of the beef you have on hand. Please,' added the other man.

Nobody had anything to say, so Loren asked, 'Can we take the feed?'

'Yes,' Sander told him.

'Where did you buy it?'

Allie said, 'Dixon True Value,' and rattled off the address and phone number.

'And the infected heifers?' asked Loren.

'Take them,' Sander said.

'We'll send a truck.'

He told them the eight animals would be gone that afternoon, as would all the feed identified as having originated in Britain. A truck followed Loren and the other man to the Sandoval store, where Jaime was given five minutes to peruse a USDA order for seizure of his stock in overseas cattle protein supplements. He handled one brand only and had no other buyers for that particular supplement. He kept a single pallet in reserve, in case the Grants ran low. This one pallet was loaded and gone by the time Allie called him to explain.

Sander's face was numb. He and his parents sat and listened to Allie on the kitchen phone. None of them had anything else to say to one another, so he decided to walk down and check the mail. He would add the newest bills to the paperwork he put off from yesterday, and compose a form letter to Argos and all their other buyers.

He was thumbing through the stack on his walk back up the drive when he came upon the distinctive parchment and gold embossing of The Paulson Gallery. Sander couldn't remember the last time he had any correspondence with Scott Jacob. What, he thought, could the man want now? Inside was a check made out to him for $3,100, the memo on which read, 'untitled, charcoal.' When Sander looked in the envelope for some explanation, he found a small handwritten note:

> My goodness ... I had no idea! More, more.
>
> SJP
>
> p.s. – should I continue to deal through Jason?

Sander ran into the house, bounded up the stairs and began hurling stuff from the closet in his studio.

From the doorway, Allie said, 'What the hell, Sander?'

He kept pulling out boxes until he could reach the back shelf. His recent artwork was there, just as he had wrapped and taped it. He pulled down the bundle and tore the paper from it, then closed the door on Allie before spreading it all out on the floor. How many had he done? Counting would do him no good. Nobody had been in that closet since he packed it full, he was sure. Was Jason passing off work under his name? He gazed absently at the far wall where his supplies sat atop cardboard boxes, some of Allie's things there now, and his eyes fell upon the wrapped wedding gift from Jason. His mother must've moved it in here from his dresser.

Sander looked back down at the charcoals scattered before him and knew exactly which one was missing. It was the angriest piece of the bunch, a Herculean man clinging to the side of an ark as it rose upon a wall of water, and it had not been among the rest when he last saw them. He flung open the door and ran back downstairs.

'When did Jason bring that wedding gift?'

'What?' said Jo.

Dalton answered, 'He came by during the reception. Around six or seven, I guess. Right as I was getting into the shower.'

'You left him alone in the house?'

'No. I sent him out to find you.'

'I never saw him, dad.'

Neither of his parents had the energy to wonder what had Sander so worked-up, and he didn't stick around long enough for explanations anyway. He went upstairs and gathered the remaining artwork from the studio, carried it straight out back to the trash barrel and set it afire. He watched the thick paper turn to embers, then flaky ash, and he stirred it with a stick to make sure no scrap survived.

Instead of going back into the house for his truck keys, he straddled the tractor, pointed it toward the hill by the pond and shifted into high gear.

12

It was well after dark when Allie saw the tractor coming back toward the barn, its dim headlamps like two luminescent balls trundling across the field. She sat on the patio and waited. Sander killed the engine and slowly made his way toward the house, mumbling to himself until he noticed her sitting there at the edge of the light spilling from the kitchen window.

'How long have you been out here?'

'I don't know,' she said.

Her face was puffy and her eyes ringed in red.

'It hurts me to see you crying, Allie, but I can't really tell you there's nothing to cry about.' He sat beside her.

'Good for you, then. Cause you missed the show. I ran out of tears.'

'I'm sorry I left. It was all I could think to do.'

'Be straight with me. You can do that.'

'Yes. I can do that.'

'Do you really talk to your dead grandparents?'

'My grandfather. And his fathers, through him,' Sander said.

'And they talk back to you.' It was somewhere between a question and an accusation, but she expected an answer.

'You know,' he said, 'how you can tell somebody's on the other end of a telephone line even if they aren't saying anything? I used to take my sketchpad up there to the hill sometimes, sit with them and watch the herd in the sunset. There were whole afternoons we wouldn't exchange a single word, but I knew they were there. Other days, I could feel them when dad and I worked the back pasture. A hundred yards away from the pond, I could sense them.'

'And tonight?'

'It's like I forgot to pay the phone bill. Nothing. It wasn't for a lack of waiting, either.'

'Okay,' she said. There was enough in those two syllables to tell Sander that his wife would only now begin to wrestle with this oddity. She did not know Sander like his mom knew his dad when they were married, and Allie could easily develop a different opinion on life with the Grants.

'Why did you burn your drawings?' she asked.

'Those were things I never intended anyone to see. I was working out stuff for myself the only way I knew how, stuff Roger had told me and things I'd learned about my own history. No real reason to keep them around, but–' He interrupted himself, 'Roger is the pastor at First Unitarian.'

'I know who he is. Why now? Why did you have to burn the stuff today?'

He pulled the folded Paulson check from his pocket and handed it to her.

'Jason took one without asking me.'

Allie glanced at the amount on the check and gave it back.

'That's a nice surprise. You didn't answer my question.'

'They weren't supposed to leave here!' He saw her jump and heard the echo of his own voice. He made an effort to calm himself. 'There were things in those charcoals–' he said. 'I had been warned to stop. In a hateful, roundabout way, I think. Warned that I was upsetting a sort of balance. I told myself I'd destroy the drawings as I made them. But I got attached, and I just wanted to see them whole. They became a sequence in my mind, a single piece. I wanted to see it through, then I was going to get rid of them all. I swore.'

'Warned by who?'

There were a couple of plain answers to that, yet Sander knew he could approach it from another direction, being honest without hurrying along her judgment.

'You go to church,' he said. 'Do you believe there would be consequences if you stood up in Mass and started shouting that the Bible was wrong, that it deceived us?'

'Yeah. I believe they would ask me to leave. Somebody might call the cops if I kept it up, I guess.'

'Higher consequences.'

'Oh. Atonement for our sins. Yes, that could be a pretty big one. I think it falls under blasphemy.'

'What if you had proof?'

'This is too much, Sander. I love you and I think you've gone through far too much today. I want you to talk to me, but you're not making any sense, baby.' She rubbed his forearm. 'You need sleep.'

'It'll all look better in the morning?'

'It'll still be a big ugly mess in the morning, but we'll deal with it. Jo gave me one of her back pills and said it would knock me out. You can have it if you want. I don't need it.'

'Just tell me, hypothetically, if you had proof that God and the church were intentionally keeping something from us, what would you do?'

'Well.' Allie withdrew her hand and thought about it. 'I'd make damn sure I had my facts straight, first off. And that I was thinking clearly. Then I'd probably talk to God about it before I started hollering in church.'

'That's a good idea,' said Sander.

'So is sleep. Can we please go to bed?'

Sander hadn't the fight in him even to argue his own sanity. Or he feared, if he tried to do so tonight, he would lose. When Allie stood and took his hand, he let her lead him inside.

Indeed, sleep was a fine idea. Many impossible things are splendid ideas. The effort to remain motionless all night, so as not to wake Allie, took more from Sander than eight hours of staring at the television. He made some decisions, though, and had ample time to evaluate and reconsider them several times over. First thing on the list for the morning was business. Grant Beef was circling the drain in a hopeless spiral, but that was no excuse to abandon professionalism. He would salvage what he could before grappling with the bigger problem.

The insurance portion of Mr Loren's plan went as expected. Ten minutes into the phone call, the company's adjuster summarily disclaimed coverage, for reason of governmental action. Sander explained that was not the case and faxed over the contact information from the USDA. The claims supervisor spoke with Mr Loren's office and whomever else, then called Sander back to tell him somebody would be out to look at the books and take a head count to determine the amount of the claim. Sander suggested they hurry.

Allie didn't know the Department of Agriculture had their own earth-moving equipment. She wasn't alone in her awe. Dalton and Jo sat on the back porch and watched as the massive dozers and track hoe excavators rumbled off a convoy of lowboy trailers, one after another. They shook the ground as they lined up abreast inside the gate. Dalton could not help but compare the sight to old World War II newsreel footage – Patton's 3rd Army preparing to meet the Germans. Except, these machines were here to plough under a bunch of cows. The equipment operators shut down their engines in succession and climbed back into the trucks that had brought them, some tipping their caps towards the patio as they passed. They would return. Dalton sipped his coffee.

It wasn't something Sander felt the need to see. At the roll-top desk in the living room, he organized bills into three stacks. There were the ones he intended to pay, come hell or high water. Next were the debts he would try to make good on, though the creditors held no collateral from the operation. Once done with the sorting, he dropped the third stack in the waste basket beside his chair. Allie watched him from the sofa.

'We can work something out with the people you can't pay right now, babe. Papa does it all the time.'

His head in the checkbook, Sander said, 'We pay those in advance. Scheduled deliveries, insurance premiums and whatnot.'

'You don't wanna at least call them and cancel your accounts? I could do that part for you.'

He sighed in disgust. 'Look outside, Allie. You think Mr Jack Loren's plan to keep this a secret is feasible? I don't care how fast they move, slaughtering six hundred head of cattle is gonna make the nightly news. I'm not expecting any delivery trucks to show up.'

She wanted a Coke from the fridge and she had to get out of the room before she snapped back at Sander, so she did take a look outside. Through the kitchen window, she saw the machines and the twin paths of chewed earth leading to each one. She saw Dalton and Jo from behind, holding hands. They were so calm out there, so incredibly strong with one another. Allie wondered what her mother-in-law was doing to console her husband, to steel him against this. Were she close enough to Jo to outright ask such a thing, then Jo might have told her before the question took shape.

Allie looked at the cold can she held and realized it was only part of what she wanted. She wanted to be standing in her own mother's kitchen, drinking a Coke in the company of people she understood, people who would talk to her. She did not want this nearly so much, however, as she wanted Sander. When she called to him to ask if she could bring him something to drink, he surprised her.

'I'm about to take a ride,' he said. 'Wanna go?'

'Sure.' She did not care where they went. From this place, *away* was a suitable destination.

When Sander pulled the truck into the lawn of First Unitarian, Allie was certain she had made the right choice in coming along. She would listen well and patiently, because she needed to know how to fix whatever Roger Carlson had screwed up in her man's head. Then she had a few words for the good pastor, too.

Jason appeared on the porch as Sander and Allie approached. He wore the look of a mourner and held his arms wide.

'I hoped you would come,' he said. 'Tough times, huh?'

Sander broke his nose with a quick right hand. There was no warning and it hardly looked vicious enough to do the damage it did. That was because Sander stood on the ground while Jason was up on the top step, making them appear the same height. When, in fact, the fist that collided with Jason's face actually outweighed his head. He dropped to the painted boards without a sound.

'Whoa!' shouted Roger. He rushed between the two men as though Jason might jump up swinging. 'I won't have that here.'

'It's over,' said Sander. 'Does he have his car?'

'Somebody dropped him off last night,' said Roger. 'He's waiting on a ride now.' Then, kneeling down, 'Are you okay?'

'Yeah,' said Jason, through bloody fingers. 'I've had worse. You got a towel or something?'

As Roger helped him to his feet, Sander said, 'Put him upstairs. I have to talk to you.'

When they went inside, Allie whispered, 'Careful, babe. We don't need you in jail.'

'Like I said, it's over. He had it coming and he knew it.'

Roger came down the stairs a few minutes later in a mood to chastise. He found Sander and Allie seated in the back pew.

'You could have seriously hurt him, Sander.'

'You bet your ass. I could've pulled his arm off and beat him with it. But I didn't.'

'No, I guess you didn't.'

'He deserves it, though. And I think you know why.'

He did know why. Sander could tell by the way he turned his attention to Allie and introduced himself.

'Alejandra Grant,' she said. 'I've heard much about you.'

'Likewise,' said Roger. Then, turning back to Sander, 'He knew he was wrong in taking your work without permission–'

'Stealing, you mean,' said Sander.

'–but he did not realize what it was he took.' Roger shot a furtive glance at Allie.

'She knows,' said Sander. 'And that's where the blame shifts to me. Rest assured, Jason got off easy compared to what's raining down on us.'

'He's leaving out my part,' Roger told Allie, 'the influence without which none of this would've happened.'

'Are you afraid?' Sander asked.

'Of you? No. If you wanted to do something to me, you would've done it.' Roger then pointed to his temple. 'Far as my head is concerned, I figure the Almighty's had ample time to do his thing as well. My culpability aside, it does no good to hurt me now. Whoever ends up with that drawing of yours will either figure out what it means, or they won't.' To Allie, he said, 'You understand, I'm not–' Roger stopped. She already disliked him. It wouldn't help matters to tell her what he *wasn't* sorry for. 'I've apologized to your husband, and I want to apologize to you. I'm sorry, Alejandra, for the hurt I've caused.'

Allie didn't have the whole picture, but the curtain was still rising.

'How much did you tell Jason?' asked Sander.

'Betrayal of a friendship is a tough sin to forgive, I said. He mitigates his behavior, in his mind, with the knowledge that you were paid well for the artwork and you need the money right now. I told him nothing else and he didn't ask, which is probably why his most pressing concern is a busted nose. So we can be reasonably sure this gallery owner in New York doesn't know what he's got, either.'

'Then why all the rest of it?' asked Sander. 'Why destroy our ranch, our livelihood? Tell me what you think I should do.'

'I've been thinking about that since Jason came to me with his story, and I just don't know. What's going on at your place is all over town. I don't see how it will stay off the national scene. Possibly nothing's required of you but to go away. Fade to obscurity, along with your art. Kinda makes sense in that light, though not completely. Doesn't keep you from doing it again later, and it could backfire. What if it draws *more* attention to your art? I'm sorry I don't have a good answer.'

'You son of a bitch,' Allie spat. 'You apologize like a rattlesnake, knowing you'll hurt somebody again.'

'You're right,' he told her. 'I hate that it caused you pain, but I do not truly repent of this.'

'Well I do,' said Sander. 'I repent meeting you, coming to this church, and everything we discussed inside it. I repent my drawings and I even repent Jason stealing one of em. Now what do I have to do so I can talk to my granddad again?'

'What?' said Roger.

'My granddad. It's like he's not there. I don't want my father going up to that hill and hearing the silence.'

'Now that's interesting.'

'You think so, Roger? Cause I think it sucks.'

Something in the air about Sander had slowly been changing, building, and must have neared critical mass. The difference in his tone and bearing was obvious now, and it wasn't a congenial shift. Both Allie and Roger felt a primitive urge to get far away from him.

'Hang on,' said Roger. 'What I meant was, it's interesting that your ancestors stopped talking to you at the same time the Lord cut me off. Have you asked your mother if she's heard from Him lately?'

'The subject didn't come up, no.'

A car pulled up outside the meeting-hall window and they heard a horn.

'That's Jason's ride. Let me get him out of here,' said Roger.

As he climbed the stairs, Allie said, 'We should go, too. This man is loco and he doesn't care about you.'

'In a minute. He knows something else.'

Jason said nothing as Roger ushered him out and shut the door.

'God isn't talking to you anymore?' Sander asked.

'Not a sound. Like you said, it's as if He's not there. And if He's not where He usually is, it means He's somewhere else.' Roger's eyebrows were up, hopeful Sander would arrive at his own conclusion. Sander didn't.

'Maybe He's answering for something,' said Roger, sitting down in front of them again. 'I figure two things to be true. First: even ruined and shamed, you can raise serious questions about the scripture. Take what I've told you, add to it the very fact that you exist, and it would make for one hell of a tent revival. Your woes might even add to your credibility with some. That's the card you hold on God. The second thing I'm sure of is that I won't live to find other Nephilim. If there are more of you out there, they're hidden so far from civilization as to preclude the vaguest rumors of their existence. You and your dad may well be the last. That's the card God holds on his council. And no startling revelation here, time is on His side.

'The rest of what's going around in my head is conjecture, but it fits. I believe God is perilously close to breaking whatever agreement He made to not harm the Nephilim. At a minimum, He's trampled all over the spirit of it. He would not have done that for some picture of a big guy hanging onto the side of Noah's boat. I think that card of yours is higher than the one I gave you. You discovered quite a bit more about the past. Am I right?'

'Yes.'

'See, I'd wager that somewhere in their agreement was a stipulation regarding who could talk to whom and for what reasons. Otherwise, why could I hear God and not his council? Why could you hear neither but, until recently, you could chat with your dead relatives?' Roger was on a roll, though Sander would not confirm anything else before hearing him out. 'The only reason I can guess they would halt communications altogether is if there was a kind of temporary cease and desist order in place. I think they're hashing something out between themselves.'

'I can't believe you're a minister,' said Allie.

'How does that help my family?' Sander asked him.

'I don't know,' Roger said once more. Allie huffed and rolled her eyes. 'What I mean is, there's no way to know until it's over. Since that could take centuries, you might as well let your descendants worry about it.'

'Come on,' Allie told Sander, 'Let's go.'

'Unless,' continued Roger, 'you're of a mind to get in the game with that high card.'

'And how would I do that?'

'First you take your wife home. I'll have things ready when you come back.'

'I don't think so,' said Allie. 'Babe, this crazy bastard just wants to make you some kind of pet martyr for his cause.'

Roger spoke to her with such sincerity Sander found it

impossible to ignore. 'Alejandra, I really don't think things will get any worse than they are. Even so, if you're not in a position to stop us, then hurting you doesn't benefit anyone.'

'By "anyone," you mean God,' she said. 'Why doesn't God twist my arm now so Sander wouldn't even consider this?'

'If He could, I think He would. That's my point. We'll be shaking things up a little, though. Any arms get twisted in the process, I'd rather they be mine.' He looked from her to Sander, then back at her for a long moment before he stood to open the door. 'You two need to talk about this. Sander, I'll be here if you decide you'd like to try it. Give me a call. It was very nice meeting you, Alejandra.'

As Allie followed Sander to the truck, she believed she had much more to say on the subject. She knew her husband well enough to realize he wasn't seeing any harm in coming back to this place. He was as vulnerable as he was desperate. Allie was convinced she could open his eyes. When she started putting together the words in her mind, however, it occurred to her that the things she was about to tell him were simply variations on a theme. She would push Sander away by continuing to rail against Roger, so she decided to settle down and reason her way through it before she spoke. Until she could attack his ridiculous assumptions and Ivy League religion from more solid ground, she would stay close to Sander to keep him from doing anything foolish.

They rode home with the windows down, the sounds of wind and traffic filling the space between them.

13

The USDA livestock disposal operation commenced one day after Sander received notification of the autopsy results and definitive diagnosis of BSE. The fifty-three-ton Caterpillar bulldozers rumbled to life and before the sun was midpoint between the eastern and western tree lines they had pushed two great depressions into the center pasture. Down into each crawled an excavator. They dug deeper, sinking steel claws into sedimentary flakes and hard-packed subsoil unknown to Grant men. They heaved out fistfuls of moist earth until their yellow arms weren't visible from the house, only the diesel smoke they exhaled as they worked. The dozers meanwhile scraped out wide, gradually sloping avenues down into the cavities.

A crew of laborers showed up after lunch. They had the look of field hands, but their collared shirts bore the same government emblem as their pick-up trucks. Which was a badge of authority, Sander concluded, for the rifles they loaded on the side lawn. Evidently, there had not been a method contrived for the mass slaughter of cattle that was more efficient than bullets. It made for compelling pictures to accompany tomorrow's news articles. For the most part, the photographers were the same ones who had come before, when the story was Sander's success, and they knew better than to leave the road onto Grant land; one small mercy.

Jo and Dalton sat on the patio again and listened to the gunfire in the distance. The crews used their trucks to corral the cattle down the avenues into the pits, the crack of their rifles like bullwhips driving the animals ahead. They would do this, Mr Loren had said, to avoid spreading diseased tissue in the pastures. Once there were forty or fifty head of cattle circling below, the riflemen took up perches around the rims and tried their best to kill each animal with a single shot. Sometimes it took three.

After each volley, one of the trucks drove down to drench the corpses with gasoline from a pump it towed. When the pyres were lit, columns of black smoke rose, then receded, over and over. A single layer at a time they burned them, else the fires would go out. It took longer than they expected and by early afternoon, neither Jo nor Dalton could tolerate more of that smell. They retreated into the house to join Sander and Allie and they decided not to watch tomorrow. Or the next day.

The house seemed to shrink around the four of them and quiet tension rose. Dalton thumbed the remote control and cursed daytime television while Jo compulsively dusted furniture and wiped down the kitchen because she thought she felt soot on every surface and it made her ill. All telephones in the house were unplugged. Jo's parents came over on the third day – unannounced, since they couldn't call – and they found they could do nothing right.

Doris answered the door when Jack Loren came by to inform them that his guys were under instruction to restore the landscape when they were done. The equipment should be gone by the end of the week. Two more days, three at most.

'It's about time,' said Doris.

Almost as if, thought Jo, she genuinely believes she has some notion of what it's like to suffer this.

School would start again soon and Sander was glad that Allie would have that reprieve. Until then, they spent much of their time upstairs. Between their bed and the studio, there was enough breathing room so that it was preferable to the scene on extended replay down below. That's how they saw it at first, when they talked to one another as little as possible. Within a day, though, roles had switched in the household. From the onset, Jo and Dalton had looked to be handling things with a coolness that baffled Allie. Their composure deteriorated as the ordeal stretched on. Above them, meanwhile, Sander began opening up to his wife – in his own way – and the young couple at last saw for themselves how a small thing can support a very big thing when both cooperate. This was despite the elephant named Roger Carlson who shared their private space. Allie maneuvered under and around the beast until she could slay it, while Sander shoved it aside.

'I talked to your mom,' confessed Allie. She combed her fingers through his chest hair beneath the sheet.

'Today?'

'No, no. I mean, I talked to her before we got married. I was really scared that, you know, how would we fit? What if we didn't fit – that was my biggest worry.' She laughed at the unintended pun.

'I thought about it, too. What did mom say?'

'That it would hurt. But not bad, and only at first. She told me not to worry. My body would adapt.'

'Has it?'

'I'm not sure "adapt" is the word. "Crave" is a good one.' She slid her hand over the hard rows of his stomach and paused at his navel.

There were slow footfalls and muffled grunts on the stairs. They both looked toward the bedroom door. It wasn't latched and the air conditioner had opened it a crack.

'That's Frank,' whispered Sander as he rolled out of bed. He slipped into his pants and told her, 'I'll see what he wants and be right back.'

'Hurry.'

Frank paused at the landing and took a drink from his glass. Sander pulled the bedroom door closed behind him and smelled the bourbon.

'You busy?' Frank asked.

Sander rubbed his bare torso and lied. 'Taking a nap.' It was a lie that even Frank should've interpreted as a hint.

'Nap later,' he said. 'I had to get away from them and I need to talk to you.' He made to pass Sander, headed for the bedroom door.

'In here,' Sander said, and led him into the studio.

Frank took the smaller chair and pointed to Allie's easel. 'What's that?'

'Allie's designing us a house. Something I can build when all this mess is over.'

'You gonna put more cows out there?' asked Frank.

It made Sander laugh. He couldn't help it. God love him, his grandpa had less tact than any man alive.

'I don't know, grandpa, we'll see. They're not done torching the old herd yet.'

'Well,' said Frank, as though about to offer some sage reflection on it all, 'your grandma aint doin so hot. Type two diabetes.

Found out last week. I'm not real clear on whether it's worse than the other types, but none of em are good.'

After a moment, Sander said, 'Alright. It can be treated, I'm sure. Have you told mom?'

'Jo has enough to worry about. And your dad – looks like you could knock him down with a feather.'

'It's not exactly a carefree milestone in my existence either.'

'You're young,' Frank told him. 'You'll bounce back. Besides, it's more you and Allie this thing concerns anyway.'

'Which thing are we talking about now?'

'I'm not in the best shape these days. I have spells where I can't remember shit. Shit that I should be able to remember. Do you see what I'm saying, son?'

'Maybe. The liquor can't be helping.'

'Get back to me on that when you've got a few more years behind you. Only reason I bring it up is because I can't take care of Doris much longer. Especially if she gets worse. I don't even know where she keeps the damn coffee filters.' Sander stared at him. Frank grew angry. 'You gonna make me have the nursing home talk with my own wife?'

'I guess not.' Then, 'Should I do it?'

'No! What you should do is offer us your bedroom once yall get this house built.' He sloshed booze on Allie's drawing and smudged the graphite when he tried to wipe it off. 'Sorry. Tell her I'm sorry.'

'It may be a year before I get that built, grandpa.' The statement was true enough, yet its purpose was to buy time while Sander flailed around for some way to avoid saying, 'This is not my house to offer you.'

'I know my daughter,' said Frank, 'and I've known Dalton longer than you. Their worry is gonna be for you and Allie. Your privacy. Do they know you're building this house?'

'No, I don't think they do. It was just something ...' He sighed and trailed off, his eyes falling from Allie's rudimentary sketch to Frank's slippers, then to the carpet between them, and coming to rest on the denim tight over his thighs.

'What?'

'We were talking about it, me and Allie. Gave us something to do to pass the time.'

'Okay, so now you know where the money will come from,' Frank said. 'We can sell our house and the few acres. Should more than pay for what you have in mind, and we have plenty more set back.'

'Yeah. I'll talk to Allie about it. Give me a little time to bring it up to mom and dad, would you?'

'Time's passing for all of us, Sander. Time is one thing that's definitely not on our side.'

'Yeah, Frank. I realize that.'

Sander watched him walk out. Frank stumbled and nearly ran into the doorjamb. He was drunker than he first appeared and his grandson excused a portion of his insensitivity on account of that. But, thought Sander, if he was incapable of anything else, he might still refrain from adding ballast to a sinking ship. In the wake of that thought came Sander's intense remorse for it. His grandparents were going through something more terrifying and absolute than what was happening in the fields outside. Here they were, though, and they were trying to help.

Sander returned to the bedroom and took his shirt from the closet door.

'Frank says nobody really feels like cooking anything tonight,' he told Allie. 'I'm gonna run a few errands in town and pick up something to eat. Any requests?'

'That's a good idea. Anything's fine with me. You want some company?'

'No, thanks. Why don't you work on your drawing? I'll be back as soon as I can.'

Sander didn't see any need to call the church before he drove out. He knew Roger had begun whatever preparations he spoke of the moment they walked out his door the other day. Like Allie, Sander had no faith in the pastor's benevolence. He had come to doubt Roger knew what an act of altruism felt like. But the man was intelligent. He was learned and he was calculating. If there was a way for Sander to slip from under God's thumb, just enough to catch his balance, Roger stood as good a chance as any at figuring it out. It could hardly hurt to try what he had in mind. On the trip over, Sander's only concern was how much Roger would want in return.

Roger didn't come out to meet him and evidently didn't know Sander was standing on the porch. This was odd because the old pier and beam foundation had settled unevenly over the years and Sander's seven hundred pounds caused the whole structure to moan. Before he could knock, he heard Roger's voice from within. Thinking there was somebody else in there, maybe Jason again, Sander turned to leave. Then he realized Roger wasn't having a conversation, but giving a lecture. He eased over to the window and peered through a gap in the curtains.

Roger was so natural at this – and later seemed indifferent as to whether anyone believed his theories – that Sander thought he simply read over a pile of notes early Sunday morning, trotted downstairs and started talking. But there he stood with chalk in hand, practicing before empty pews; backing up and trying different turns of phrase and giving himself verbal pointers on timing.

Sander watched for a minute or two, then stepped back to the door and knocked.

'Damn,' said Roger when he opened the door. He left it ajar as he hurried into the kitchen, calling over his shoulder, 'Have a seat.'

Sander sat where he always did, the only pew that would accommodate his legs. Beside him was a reel-to-reel tape recorder, about the size of his mother's sewing machine, with a microphone atop it. On the far side of the apparatus were several steno pads and a cup full of pencils. He checked to see if the tape recorder was running. It was not.

'I know you said to call,' Sander shouted, 'but I was in the neighborhood. You record your lectures?'

Roger returned from the kitchen with the same quickstep pace. He carried an armload of towels and his bottle of morphine.

'No problem,' he said. 'The machine is for you. I was ready except for this stuff.' He placed the towels and his medicine bottle on the pew in front of Sander and sat down beside them. 'I don't intend to be interrupted this time. Could you hand me those pads and pencils, please?' Sander obliged. Roger glanced at the front door as though he was considering locking it, then flipped open a pad and said, 'Push the record button on that thing.'

'I'm not sure what we're doing here.'

'Please,' Roger implored, 'push the button before you say anything else. Then I'll explain.'

Sander did. The reels turned slowly and made no noise.

Roger dated his tablet and scrawled two lines in some kind of shorthand.

'Here's the deal,' he told Sander. 'We're about to get somebody's attention. Simply by intent, I think we already have. What we're saying is recorded,' he pointed to the reels, 'and I'm making a written backup.' He paused to scratch down another note. 'Man reigns sovereign over history, Sander. I think I told you this already. Whether we skew it, lie about it, or lay it down as it happened, it is our right alone. Once it's recorded, only we can destroy it. So it's important that you keep talking, no matter what happens. Got it?'

'Not really. What is it we're talking about?'

'Whatever needs saying. If I might make a suggestion, I'd start with just that: what you need.'

'What I need ...' Sander felt a twinge of awkwardness and asked, 'Am I supposed to be talking to God, here?'

'The recorder doesn't care how you say it. Talk to me, if you like.'

'Alright,' he began. 'Several years ago, my granddad told me this story about his first mule. He bought the thing young and he grew attached to it pretty quick. For whatever reason, the bulls didn't like this little mule and the mule wouldn't stay away from them. Granddad figured it would learn soon enough and things would sort themselves out. He was fifteen, not much older than me, when one of the bulls finally got a horn in that mule. A vet came out, took one look and said there was nothing to be done. The mule had to be put down. The vet asked my granddad, "You want me to do it while I'm here?" Granddad was torn up over it, but he turned to the doctor and said, "Why would I ask you to kill my mule?" He carried the animal to the woods and snapped its neck.

'Then, just here recently, granddad sorta compared us to mules. I doubt he connected the two stories, but I did. So, what do I need?' asked Sander. 'I need to cut through the shit. If there's nothing to be done here but put us down, somebody ought to step up and take care of his own business. Otherwise, leave us be. I don't want any favors. I want nothing. No miracles. No more pestilence. Nothing.'

'Is that it?' Roger asked him. Sander's mindset was fatalistic and driven by a simmering rage, but Roger knew he needed to say these things – and they served a greater good. The man who begins bargaining with rational demands leaves with less than he could've gained.

'Naw, that aint it. I'll absolve God from His promise not to harm me. Next time He feels the urge to inflict pain, He can bring it straight on. If my wife gets one of your nosebleeds,' he told Roger, 'or ends up hunched over in the yard, I'll start pushing down churches and I won't stop.' Hearing his anger fall flat in an empty room, Sander chuckled to himself. 'Did I just say pestilence? Nobody's listening, Roger.'

'I feel quite sure you have an audience. Would you like to talk more about what your grandfather said?'

'Why not.'

Sander's memory was as sharp as ever. He recounted what Will had told him, almost verbatim, without supposition or conclusion of his own. It meshed neatly with what Roger already knew and so required no clarification, but Roger occasionally interjected verbal footnotes for the record. When he asked questions, even leading ones, Sander assured him no answers were forthcoming. He told Roger again and again to just listen.

When he was done, Sander looked at his watch.

'Do you have somewhere to be?' asked Roger.

'Yeah. I told them I would bring back supper. Can I use your phone?'

'In the kitchen.'

'I need to order some pizza,' Sander said as he stood. 'Want me to turn off the recorder?'

'No. There's plenty of tape.'

Sander made the call and returned to his seat, resting his elbows on his knees. He was obviously eager to wrap things up. 'I've got another twenty minutes, but that's about it. What's next?'

'Well, you were clear about what you want. And it's obvious what kind of doubt you could cast on the canon of theology with your information. Since we're getting no response, I assume somebody's waiting to hear what you're willing to offer.'

'Besides not holding tent revivals?' Sander said.

Roger smiled. 'In addition to that.'

Sander couldn't have felt any more foolish, nor any less adequate than he did at that moment. When he came here thinking he had nothing to lose, he neglected to consider the measure of his pride and the value his people placed on privacy. Though he couldn't explain it, he was somehow compelled to see the thing through. Seemed like leaving here now, without another word, would worsen the deeds already done.

'What?' he asked Roger. 'My family is falling apart. We've got no livestock left and we'll be broke in a matter of weeks. Reckon He would rather have a pound of flesh or my firstborn child?'

Roger raised his eyebrows and stopped writing. He said, 'I know you're skeptical about what we're doing. That's fine. Some things don't require your belief. But please listen to me when I say: do not offer anything here that you can't bear to lose.'

Sander turned off the recorder fifteen minutes later. 'Still got no answer,' he said.

While he finished his notes, Roger asked, 'Are you absolutely sure we didn't?' He looked up to see courage in the eyes staring back at him. He didn't know what he would've preferred to see, but courage implied fear, which meant the young man was sure of little. Roger regretted that he would leave the church in that state. He wished there was something he could do about it. He had come to respect Sander, nearly to the point of awe considering how furiously all of this had been piled on his shoulders. Had Sander been any member of the congregation, Roger would've reassured him, because that's what pastors are taught to do: encourage people to rely on their faith for stability in these situations.

These situations, though? Possibly he had missed that day but, as far as he could remember, seminary offered no guidance on counseling giants. He was equipped with many a means for explaining the depth of God's love, the completeness of His devotion to the salvation of man in the aftermath of what deplorable things beset them. Not one platitude or parable did he have to ease the impact on someone God holds in abomination. He vaguely remembered telling Sander something along these lines and he didn't feel like doing it again. That left only silence, as anything from his repertoire of shibboleth would have been insulting.

Sander pointed to the tape reels. 'You're gonna publish all that. What then?'

'Oh, no I'm not. I figure I deserve a normal lifespan as much as you do. The decision to share this information is entirely separate from the act of recording it.'

'Pretty slick, Roger. Got yourself some leverage there. If it works, that is. I wonder what's to stop me from taking all of it.'

'Take it!' he said, extending his three tablets. 'I can't think of safer hands to leave it in, but I wouldn't really call it leverage.' Sander didn't reach for the tablets and Roger dropped them beside the recorder. 'In case you change your mind.'

Sander nodded.

'We've made our best play,' said Roger. 'Whether you realize it or not, I was the only one with a choice in the matter. Could've walked away from you, my research, and all the rest of it any time I wanted. The problem there being, I couldn't *want* to. Your family, on the other hand, was caught squarely in the middle of something you didn't understand. That was the case long before I came around. But you made a deal here tonight, Sander. So this stuff isn't leverage for you anymore. It's more like a liability. Seriously, I would take it if I were you. Just keep in mind that somebody else needs to know where to find it, and nobody ever needs to see it.'

'Keep it,' Sander said, rising to leave. 'I just needed to talk. Use it to write your new Bible or throw it out with the garbage. I'm glad your headache didn't come back.'

'Me too.'

His hand on the doorknob, Sander paused. 'I can't remember how many times I've said this, but I don't think we need to see each other again. Do you?'

'I think, at this point, it would be wise not to. I won't be staying in Dixon any longer than it takes to pack my things. Goodbye, Sander.'

14

Dalton was so glued to his big chair in the living room that he didn't even get up when Jo called 'They're leaving!', didn't join the rest of the family to watch the USDA trucks pull away with their machinery. He didn't change the television channel anymore when random news stories trickled in about the public health crisis narrowly averted in East Texas, and those eventually ceased. It was the last straw for Jo when, days later, he asked her to bring him his dinner. He didn't feel like eating at the table tonight.

'Your plate will be where it always is,' she said.

At the table, she tried to free him from his self-imposed incarceration.

'You really ought to go out to the pasture and see what they've done.'

'I know what they did, Jo. Everybody in the country knows what they did.'

'For what it's worth,' Sander interjected, 'Mr Loren was right. A lot of fuss, but since there was no beef recall, prices have remained fairly stable.'

'I mean,' Jo told Dalton, 'take a walk out there. They put it all back like they said they would, and they seeded it with grass. It doesn't even smell anymore.'

'That's something,' he said. 'The land's worthless to anybody who can read or watch TV, but maybe some new grass will help.'

Jo absorbed his sarcasm. She was dead set on getting him out of the house, convinced it would do him good. 'Have you been to the hill by the pond since all of this started?'

Allie looked at Sander. He was frozen, his fork buried in a pile of macaroni and his mouth closed so tightly she thought the muscles in his jaw might break the skin.

'No,' said Dalton. 'I wouldn't know what to say.'

'Kinda selfish, don't you think? Maybe Will has something to tell you, honey. At least give him some–' Jo saw Sander's face and stopped.

A moment passed. Forks chirped on plates. Ice rattled in glasses.

'I'll go,' said Dalton. 'Tomorrow.'

There it was, the day Sander knew would come. His mom was right, the exercise on the way out there probably would invigorate dad. Then the awful silence would crush him. Sander relaxed. It was over, or it would be very soon. Dalton would go out there and discover for himself the full extent of their loss in this debacle; which was, present company excluded, total. Surely it would drive his dad to the bottom. In a way, that could be preferable to this. The one good thing about hitting bottom is that you're not falling anymore.

Another thought occurred to Sander. He knew his dad's habit of sorting things out, working through his concerns on the walk to the hill. Sander had always just plopped down and started rambling, but Dalton liked to present things in a quasi-formal manner to Will. Possibly it was a son's respect for his father.

Or, as it sometimes seemed to Sander, his dad was still seeking Will's approval. Hell, maybe they had always talked that way to one another. Regardless, Dalton might hang on to whatever he figured out for himself, after he recovered from the fact that he had nobody to share it with any longer.

Allie helped Jo clear the table then led Sander to bed. In the past weeks, sex had become their escape and their solace. Having both been virgins when they wed, they seemed to concur on the special gravity of intercourse. If they could know one another as nobody else ever had or would, and if they could enjoy so completely the feel and weight and smell of their bodies together, then what subject of conversation could be difficult to broach? So sex was also their icebreaker, even when the ice was thin enough to shatter in a breeze, or there was no ice for miles around.

Afterward, they talked for a long time that night. Sander told her all his worries over what would come tomorrow. It so happened Allie had some insight, recently acquired, into how he might prepare himself to act when his dad got back to the house.

'Listen,' she told him. 'They always say that. "Just listen." I don't know how it is with other men, but with yall that's not enough. You'll find yourself sitting there like I did, listening to the ceiling fan. You have to sort of gently demand that he talk to you. Does that make sense? Claim your right to hear what's hurting him, and do it before he decides that he's better off handling it alone.'

'We're not like that, are we?'

'Babe, you people clam up like a mob boss in a courtroom. It's hard to tell if you understand English sometimes. I'm saying you have to get him to open up before he's turned the lock, or he never will. Not about this.'

'Yeah, I see what you're saying. I'm not sure how far to go,' said Sander, 'when he asks me why it happened.'

'Why would he ask you that?' She rose up on one elbow and poked him in the chest. 'If you say anything to him about that crazy man at the church, I'll hit you with a piece of furniture. I'm not kidding. Your father won't blame you for this. Leave it alone.'

'I wasn't really talking about blame,' he said. 'Kiss me.'

Dalton was gone right after breakfast. Sander and Allie hadn't closed their eyes until midnight, and Sander guessed his wife was sleeping late. He decided there would be no better time to talk to Jo about Doris and Frank.

'Mom,' he said, 'could you sit down with me for a minute?'

She did, dishtowel on her shoulder. 'I hope this is what your father needs,' she said. 'If not, I don't know what else to do.'

'I'll talk to him when he gets back, see if I can help him.' She nodded, grateful. 'Not that you need any more to think about, but I've noticed grandma Doris isn't getting around any better.'

'Dad said something to you, didn't he?' asked Jo. 'He's a sneaky old cuss. I was planning to have a discussion with them about it soon. I'll do it today or tomorrow. Take them around to some of the assisted living places.'

'Don't put them in a nursing home, mamma. I've got an idea.'

'Not nursing homes,' she scoffed. 'They aren't that old. I'm talking about those communities where they've got people on staff to check on the residents, help them. Your grandparents would have their own place.'

'Yeah, I think those staff people are called nurses. Anyway, has Allie told you she's designing us a house? I'm planning to build it here on the ranch, maybe fence off a little plot in one of the back corners. Allie likes the woods.'

'And your grandpa Frank likes your bedroom. Yall have this all figured out, don't you?'

'He mentioned it.'

'So you want me to play nurse,' she said. 'Now I see why he sent you.'

This wasn't going at all as Sander anticipated. He suspected there was a little cunning in Frank's approach.

'Nobody sent me. We were just talking. He says they have plenty of savings. If they need a nurse, let them hire one. There may come a time ...' he began. 'I mean, down the road it might not be practical for them to stay here. But don't you wanna give it a try?'

'I'll think about it.' They both heard the upstairs toilet flush for the third time in the space of a few minutes. 'Go check on her,' said Jo. 'I think she's sick.'

'She's okay. Had a little stomach bug for the past couple of days. She says it's getting better.'

Jo smiled. 'Uh-huh. And when does this bug rear its head most? In the morning, when her blood sugar is low?'

'I guess. I don't know. Why?'

They heard Allie coming down the stairs.

'I'd ask her, if I were you. Could be you've got better things to worry about than where your grandpa sleeps.'

Allie was ravenous. Sander took his mother's meaning, but he didn't have a game plan for the discussion she had suggested. It hit him out of nowhere and he wasn't sure what he wanted to hear when he started asking questions. So he cleared his throat with every sip of coffee and watched as Jo cooked more eggs and bacon and his wife kept eating.

When she'd had enough, Jo said, 'Oh, for Pete's sake.' She took the phone book from a kitchen drawer and turned to the page of local physician listings. She put it beside Allie's plate and said, 'Marshal Talbot is the best around. He delivered Sander.' Then she put a pan of sweet rolls on the table and told Allie, 'I'm going to get dressed. You keep eating, hon. You're gonna need it.'

Allie decided to skip school. She made the call at nine o'clock.

Sander grew more worried by the minute as he fidgeted on the patio and scanned the pasture for any sign of Dalton, ready to read his gait and judge the level of dismay or confusion. It was still very odd to see all that land with no cattle on it. Was it possible, he wondered, that his dad was still sitting up there waiting? Sander tried to remember how long he had talked to the tree until he gave it up. He was about to start walking that way himself when he saw his father striding toward the house. His pace was so slow. It seemed to take another hour for him to reach the gate. Sander focused on his face. Could it be, he thought, that his dad actually looked less troubled than when he left?

'Hey, son,' he said as he passed Sander.

'Dad?'

'Yeah.'

'How did it go?'

'Your mom was right. She normally is. That's just what I needed.' He opened the door and remembered something else: 'Your granddad said to come see him. He wants to make sure you're okay, I think.'

Sander was okay, he felt reasonably sure of that much about himself, but either his dad was losing it, or – what? He shot an involuntary glance toward the window, where Allie had been standing with the telephone.

When he found her upstairs, she was showered and getting dressed.

She asked him the same question he had asked his father. 'How did it go?'

'They apparently had a good long chat.'

'Oh no, babe. Do you think he sat up there all that time talking to himself?'

'I don't know.'

She looked at her watch. 'We'll figure something out on the way. The lady at the doctor's office says he'll make an opening around noon.'

'Today?'

'Yes, today. Get ready and I'll meet you downstairs.'

'I'm ready.'

'You're not going like that, are you?'

'I'm going exactly like this. I don't know of any other way to go.' Sander's head was a whorl of confusing thoughts. When he tried to concentrate on a single one, they moved faster.

'At least put on a good shirt,' said Allie.

Dr Talbot didn't get to them before lunch. Their fingerprints were on every page of every magazine in the building. It was going on two o'clock when the nurse called Allie's name. Sander wondered whether he was supposed to go back there, but Allie took his hand and pulled him along as she went.

'How exciting,' Dr Talbot said, when he came into the exam room. 'Another Grant baby. Allie, I'm Marshal.' He shook her hand, then turned to Sander, 'And I know you.' He pointed to his face, 'This ugly mug is the first thing you ever saw.'

'I remember,' Sander told him, hunched over beneath the fluorescent light. 'Ceilings seemed higher back then.'

'Right. Well, I'm as experienced in this as anybody alive. But you have to know, Allie, there's no book to study on the Grants. We learn as we go, to some extent. I suppose you've been told as much.'

'Yes.'

'Okay. Just so you know. I can give you some idea what to expect, based on Jo's medical history. When were you two planning the pregnancy?'

Allie looked at Sander, then back to the doctor.

'I think I'm pregnant now,' she said. 'Maybe a few weeks?'

'Well, then.' The doctor put his folio on the counter and washed his hands. 'I see. Guess I didn't understand the message.' He motioned for Allie to lie back on the table and he smoothed the blouse over her flat belly. 'Hmmm.'

'What?'

'Have you had a test, or did you just miss your period?'

'Morning sickness.'

Dr Talbot said, 'Allie, we don't normally use sonography in the first two months of pregnancy unless there's a problem. Bleeding, that kind of thing. This is only because, in average cases, it doesn't tell us much of anything at this stage. It can give us an age of the pregnancy, though. There's no harm to the fetus, or embryo, whichever the case may be.'

'What does that mean?' Sander wondered.

'If you're agreeable, I'd like to get an ultrasound picture and see exactly how far along we are.'

The doctor waited while they exchanged glances, shrugged, and Allie nodded.

'It'll take ten minutes,' he said. 'Let me get you a gown.'

Dr Talbot left while she changed. Sander asked Allie why he excused himself.

'He's gonna see everything you've got down there pretty soon anyway.' Then, 'Maybe it's because I'm in here.'

Allie, in turn, asked him why he thought the doctor was doing an ultrasound. It seemed to her that he might be thinking there was some problem.

'I know you're not honestly expecting me to have an opinion,' said Sander.

'I'm worried, babe.'

Sander was thinking of what he could give her besides his token warranty that everything was alright. He was sorry for being sarcastic. He had decided to say nothing and soothe her with a kiss, but the doctor knocked and opened the door before he got the chance.

'Okay,' said Talbot. 'Lie back for me.'

He rolled a cart to the side of the examination table and raised Allie's gown to a pleated scrunch beneath her breasts. Sander saw her pink lace panties against her dark skin and thought how beautiful his wife was, and how lucky a man was he.

Dr Talbot said, 'This might be cold,' as he squirted yellowish-clear jelly on her abdomen. Sander thought that was rather disgusting. The doctor turned on the little computer screen and said, 'Let's see who's in there, shall we?'

The screen on the cart flashed gray, then displayed an undulating triangular image of who knew what. Sander thought he might be looking at a slice of the pizza he'd brought home the other night, whole and moving around in Allie's stomach.

'Okay. Alright,' Talbot said, as he slid the thing around on Allie.

'Can you tell us what we're seeing?' Sander asked.

'I can't see the screen,' said Allie.

Dr Talbot said, 'Sure. Sorry,' and he rotated the monitor where Allie could have a look. 'Okay, what we have here,' he made a circle on the screen with two fingers on his free hand, 'is a normal, healthy gestational sac. We can't tell much more than that at this point.'

'Oh,' Allie sighed. 'You had me scared. Seemed like you thought something was wrong.' She squeezed Sander's hand and smiled up at him.

'I might not have made myself clear,' Talbot said. 'Have you seen another obstetrician already?'

'No. Why?'

'This,' he pointed again, 'is the classic picture of a healthy three-to-five-week pregnancy. A normal pregnancy. Normal in every aspect.' Dr Talbot shut off the machine and looked from one to the other of them until he saw the news register in their faces. 'Not what you were expecting, I take it. I thought that might be the case.'

On the drive home, Allie's first three questions were: Has this ever happened before? Does this mean I might have a girl? And are you disappointed? At least, Sander thought that was the order they came out. The only definitive answer he could provide without hesitation was the last. No. Bald shock was not the same as disappointment.

As for the rest, well, it hadn't happened in a thousand years. Sander knew that from talking to Will. He seriously doubted it had happened before, but he couldn't be sure. And, yes, a daughter might be in the cards for them. Several, if logic held. He wasn't sure how much of that he verbalized, as he was waiting for a specific question – another for which he had a ready and true answer. It didn't come.

Sander couldn't help but recall Allie's words from last night, when they were talking about Dalton's trip to the hill. Over and over he heard her saying, 'Your father won't blame you for this.' He had little doubt that his wife was correct in that regard. Though he may have stirred it up, he didn't feel anyone could rightfully lay at his doorstep any part of an argument that predated the Lord's covenant with Abraham. However, the deal he made only days ago, when he was dubious that anyone besides Roger was listening, that was wholly on him. What he gained aside, and however others might judge the bargain, what was taken in exchange had been proffered by Sander Grant.

Allie's rush of excitement led to a bit more honesty than she would otherwise have volunteered. No matter. She could live with admitting to a shade of disappointment. After all, she had spent so many hours and more than a few whole nights dreaming what it would be like to have such a big boy. What she hadn't especially been looking forward to was the discomfort involved. So she admitted she wouldn't be missing that, or the speed at which Grant babies were known to develop. She was looking forward to her eight more months to get ready and, hopefully, finish her junior year of high school.

They agreed on one thing before they reached the house. Sander had to break the news to his folks. Not the pregnancy – they figured Jo already told Dalton that – but the real news. Sander said he had a couple of weeks to tell them before they would be expecting Allie to show. He figured the more time he gave his dad, the better. Allie could share the joy with her parents however and whenever she wanted. The two families hardly ever talked anymore and nobody in the Sandoval house had any idea how big Allie should be at a certain date.

15

Dalton's spirits were greatly buoyed. He didn't know of a time when there had been three generations of them alive at once. He could hardly wait to ask Will if it had ever happened before.

'Don't worry,' he said to Sander. 'I'll let you tell him first.'

That wasn't something Sander was all too anxious to do. He didn't know whether Will and the rest of them felt anything amiss during those days when they were cut off from one another. If they had, there would be questions. Sander no longer doubted Will was talking again, and he would have to make his way to the hill soon. He would not lie to his granddad, though, and he wasn't prepared to come out with the whole truth.

Meanwhile, the pregnancy made it much easier for Jo to have her overdue chat with Frank and Doris. Obviously Sander and Allie would be building their own place now, and they needed to get moving as time had become an issue. When the dark clouds over Dalton had parted, Jo first mentioned to him the idea of moving her parents to the ranch. It so happened that he had long taken their role in that capacity as a given, and did not resent it.

It was the following morning, a Saturday, when Jo decided to pay her parents a visit and get things rolling. Dalton had one last thought on the matter.

'Your dad is gonna have to cut back on the drinking,' he said. 'Especially with a kid around.'

Jo agreed. 'Will you help Sander build the house?'

'Yeah. More of a cabin they've got planned, really. I'll throw out a few ideas to make it comfortable for three.'

'Good. It has to come along pretty quick, though.'

'We're starting this afternoon, honey. Don't worry about it.'

Jo didn't. What she worried about was how she would tell her mother that all the old furniture she loved would have to go. Jo didn't want her place turned into a granny house.

She kissed Dalton, grabbed her purse, and said, 'Yall have fun. I might be gone a while.'

The price of lumber seemed to skyrocket, thought Sander, when you had no expectation of making back the money you dropped on it. The truck shook as McCoy's forklifts loaded the flatbed. He looked over at Allie and she was grinning. He returned her smile, attempting to conceal thoughts about his savings account balance. It was enough to build what Allie had envisioned, and then some. Yet, Sander knew his dad was right. The place simply wouldn't be big enough. Even after Sander had reminded Allie to raise the ceilings to twelve feet, double the size of the doors, and include at least one shower and toilet he could actually use, the house was too small by half. This load of materials would only get them started.

'What's on your mind, babe?' she asked.

Why hide it, he thought. They would dig the foundation

and she would notice right away it was much bigger than the measurements on the drawing.

'Frank offered to help out with the cost,' he told her. 'They'll have some extra when they sell their place. It bothers me to take it, but I reckon we'll have to.'

'We'll pay it back,' she said, and patted his thigh.

How?, he thought, but kept that bit to himself.

It was nice to see Dalton on the tractor again. Sander was done uprooting the few trees too close to the homesite and watched his dad steer a wide arc around the disturbed earth in the center pasture. He treated the ground over his herd as hallowed. As he neared, the wind shifted and flattened Dalton's shirt against his thin frame. Sander turned away and began filling stump holes with the shovel.

They had the earth leveled and all the corners staked out well before dark. Dalton told his son to take the tractor back and bring up the trailer of materials.

'That's alright, dad. This is enough for today. You can ride back. I feel like walking.'

'Are you sure you wouldn't rather put a concrete slab under this thing? It's gonna sound like thunder when you walk across the floor.'

'I'll reinforce the beams,' said Sander. He knew well the price of concrete. 'The sound doesn't bother me.'

'I wasn't talking about it bothering *you*,' Dalton said, then started the tractor and headed home.

It took them a while to get rolling Sunday morning, what with discussion still underway regarding Dalton's opinions on the design, specifically the elements thereof that he believed his son would live to regret. Allie was supposed to be out here with snacks and supervision. Sander wondered where she was. If and when she arrived, his dad would shut up about her plans.

Once they began, construction moved along at a steady, albeit average, pace. Sander had picked up a lot of pointers from watching Javier and Miguel, and he remembered all his costly mistakes when he had tried to help them. Dalton worked hard but Sander took it upon himself to double his effort. He would tell his dad how he wanted something done – these joists spanning those piers, with webbing staggered here, here, and here – then he would rush to grab the boards before Dalton could lift them himself.

'Son,' he said, 'if you want to build the thing yourself, just tell me. I've got other things I can be doing.'

'Sorry.'

Sander kept a close eye on him, and feigned fatigue once every couple of hours so they would have to take a break. Allie and Jo brought them lunch and they were impressed with the progress. Dalton wasn't.

When the women left, he told Sander, 'You can keep dragging ass if you want, but I intend to get the rafters up today.'

By dark, the skeleton of the house was done. Dalton didn't seem much the worse for it, so Sander quit worrying. He was now looking forward to having the outside completed in a week. Accomplishment for its own sake, he guessed, because there wasn't a list of things clamoring for their attention. They were slowly getting used to seeing two square miles of vacant land, but they had no idea yet how they would feed themselves off it.

Every time the subject came up, it was, 'I reckon we'll figure something out.'

'Sure we will, don't you think?'

'We always do.'

'Yeah.'

They switched roles, but the conversation didn't change.

Day three started about the same. They joked with one another as they began work and things were chugging right along before the dew was dry. Dalton tossed sheets of plywood up to the roof as fast as Sander could nail them down. The early autumn sun crested the treetops in short order and Sander noticed his dad was moving a little slower. He peered over the eave and saw Dalton was sweating from cap to boots, so he nailed the last bit of roof decking and climbed down for some water.

They sat together on the rough-framed floor of the house and didn't say much. Dalton seemed enough like his old self the previous day that Sander had toyed with the idea of telling him about his grandchild. He lay in bed last night and imagined the scene several different ways. He didn't talk to Allie about it. She was asleep, anyway.

Now, though, when he looked over at Dalton, it appeared his dad already had something on his mind, something that troubled him. It didn't seem like the time for surprises.

Instead, he stood and told him, 'Come on. We're wasting daylight.'

Dalton didn't get up. 'I wish you would talk to your granddad.'

'I know. I will. I'll go tonight.' He gave his father's boot a little kick, 'Let's get the sheathing on.'

'Nah. Go now.'

'What?'

'Go on over and talk to him now. He misses you and he hasn't even heard the news.'

'Are you serious?'

'Yeah. Please. I'll get started on the walls.'

When Dalton rose, he was done talking. He started toward the stack of sheathing, putting on his gloves. Sander could see the top of the tree on the hill from here. He knew, what with the inevitable questions and even his most cursory answers, he'd be an hour there and back, minimum. Shit. At least it would be over, he thought.

To his amusement, Sander found himself organizing a prepared speech with each step, pondering the order of things he would say to Will, and thereby came to understand why his dad did the same thing. This is what you do, he decided, when you would rather not say anything at all. Allie had nutshelled their preferred manner of dealing with difficult subjects. Silence.

He was a hundred yards past the truck when he heard falling lumber behind him. He couldn't see much of the structure, so he trotted back to find out what his dad had dropped. When he saw Dalton on the ground, he sprinted.

'Dad!'

The big man tried to push himself up, but his hands found no purchase. He had taken down a stud wall when he fell and now feebly struggled to get free of it. His arms buckled and his head dropped on the pine. Sander rolled him off the boards and onto his back.

'Dad? Can you open your eyes?'

'No, son. I can't.'

'You want some water or–' Sander realized his father's mouth didn't move when he said that. His face was slack. Sander shook him anyway. 'Dad?'

'Take me to the hill,' Sander heard him say, 'and go get your mother.'

Sander promised himself he wouldn't walk into the house crying, and he fought for that tiny grace, hoping he might have time to hug his mother and support her before he broke her heart. He would've made it, too, if he had gone straight in and not stopped at the barn to load a shovel in the truck.

Jo was stitching a hole in their duvet cover when it jarred her. She felt Dalton fall with such a crushing finality that she could no longer remember what she was doing. She sat on the sofa with needle and thread raised, focused on nothing in particular, until she heard the door open.

Sander walked around the corner, eyes pouring, and rather than supporting Jo, he crumpled to his knees and let his head fall in her lap.

'Is your daddy gone?'

'Yes,' said Sander, his voice muffled in the quilted feathers.

'Is he on the hill?'

'Yes.'

'Well, get up,' she said, coaxing his shoulders and smoothing his hair. 'Come on now, get up. Let's go.'

Sander thought he heard her breath hitch once on the drive out, but she turned toward the side window and when he saw her face again there was no sign of a tear. When they arrived, Jo walked beneath the tree and laid in the grass beside Dalton. She took off his cap and she kissed him. She talked to him, the same as she always did, and she didn't seem to know, or care, whether they were alone. She told him he was so beautiful, and so strong, and he was her giant.

Sander took the shovel and started digging. He stopped after a while to wipe his nose, unsure if he should interrupt his mother to tell her what Dalton was saying. Jo sensed it.

'Tell me what he said, Sander.'

'He said,' Sander began, trying hard to get it out, '"Jo, honey, I love you and I wish you could hear me."'

'I can,' she whispered and kissed him again. 'I'll come up here and have my coffee with you every morning. Don't ever stop talking to me, Dalton.'

Sander wanted to allow them privacy, so he put his back into the work and dug with fury. When he was chest deep beneath the turf, he pushed himself out. Jo squeezed Dalton's hand and stood.

'He said something right then, didn't he?' she asked.

'Yeah. He said it's not scary and he's in good company.'

'Something else. You started to grin.'

'He said roll him in and cover him up.'

She looked at her husband and said, 'That's crass, honey.' But she couldn't deny a little smile. She told her son, 'I'm not any help with this. I'll see you back at the house.' She started off across the field.

'It's a long walk, mamma.'

'It's a long cry, son.'

Sander eased his dad into the hole and filled it, still working on how to tell the man something important. He looked at his watch. Allie would be home soon. Frank and Doris and the Sandovals would come over tonight to funeralize. Jo would no doubt cook for all of them.

'I hope I didn't knock your house down,' his dad said. 'You should hire somebody to help you get it done.'

'I'll finish in plenty of time,' Sander told him.